Open for Debate

Security v. Privacy

These premises
are under
CCTV
surveillance

Open for Debate

Security v. Privacy

Rebecca Stefoff

Marshall Cavendish
Benchmark
New York

*With thanks to Danny Hayes, assistant professor,
Department of Political Science, Senior Research Associate,
Campbell Public Affairs Institute, Maxwell School
of Citizenship and Public Affairs, Syracuse University,
for his expert review of the manuscript.*

Marshall Cavendish Benchmark
99 White Plains Road
Tarrytown, NY 10591-9001
www.marshallcavendish.us

Copyright © 2008 by Rebecca Stefoff

All Internet sites were available and accurate when sent to press.

Library of Congress Cataloging-in-Publication Data
Stefoff, Rebecca, [date]
Security v. privacy : open for debate / by Rebecca Stefoff.
p. cm.
Includes bibliographical references and index.
ISBN 978-0-7614-2578-6
1. Privacy, Right of—United States—Juvenile literature.
2. Civil rights—United States—Juvenile literature.
3. National security—United States—Juvenile literature.
4. Electronic surveillance—United States—Juvenile literature.
5. Terrorism—United States—Prevention—Juvenile literature.
I. Title. II. Title: Security versus privacy.

JC596.2.U5S83 2008
323.44'80973—dc22
2007009112

Photo research by Lindsay Aveilhe/Linda Sykes
Picture Research, Inc., Hilton Head, SC

Peter Macdiarmid/Getty Images: Cover, 2–3; Mark M. Lawrence/Corbis: 6;
Kim Kulish/Corbis: 11; Getty Images: 19, 89; Hulton Archive/Getty Images: 24;
Time and Life Pictures/Getty Images: 33; AP/Wide World Photos: 42, 56, 72, 115;
Ramin Talale/Corbis: 45; Reuters: 61, 117; Bettmann/Corbis: 100; Najilah Feanny/
Corbis: 104; Paul Howell/Getty Images: 106; Bob Johns expresspictures.co.uk/Alamy: 121.

Publisher: Michelle Bisson
Art Director: Anahid Hamparian
Series Designer: Sonia Chaghatzbanian

Printed in China

1 3 5 6 4 2

Contents

Attack on the United States   7

Privacy and the Law   23

Patriotic Protection or Loss of

Civil Liberties?   41

Under Surveillance   70

Students, Schools, and Safety   98

Privacy and Security in the Future   113

Notes   124

Further Information   131

Bibliography   134

Index   136

WARNING

24HR CCTV

Recording & Monitoring

nauthorised access, theft or vandalis
will result in prosecution.

Kapture.n

SMOKE FILLS THE AIR AND DEBRIS CLOGS THE STREETS AFTER THE TERRORIST ATTACK ON NEW YORK CITY IN 2001. THE DISASTER SHOOK AMERICANS' SENSE OF SECURITY ON THEIR OWN SOIL, LAUNCHING A DEBATE OVER HOW BEST TO PROTECT THE NATION.

1
Attack on the United States

At a quarter to nine on a weekday morning, the financial hub of New York City hums with energy. Throngs of people navigate the sidewalks on their way to jobs in the office buildings that line the streets like canyon walls. The air is filled with the honking of car horns, the rumble of buses and delivery trucks, and thousands of hurrying footsteps.

On one bright, blue-sky morning in September 2001, commuters who glanced up saw an eerie sight: a huge aircraft flying unusually low overhead. The next instant the ground shuddered as though shaken by a slight earthquake and people heard a sound they will never forget: the explosive crash of an American Airlines Boeing 767 jet slamming into the side of one of New York's two tallest skyscrapers, the north tower of the World Trade Center (WTC). Its twin, the south tower, would be hit seventeen minutes later.

Before that day was over, thousands of Americans would die—and hundreds would perform acts of heroism and self-sacrifice—in a wide-ranging, carefully planned terrorist attack on the United States. Two immense skyscrapers, symbols of American capitalism, would topple.

The Pentagon in Washington, D.C., seat of the nation's armed-forces command and symbol of its military might, would also come under attack. Americans would find themselves at war with a shadowy, elusive enemy. They would also find themselves at the beginning of a debate about how best to protect the nation from terrorism. That debate is part of a larger question: What must we do to safeguard the American people and nation? Or, to put it another way, how much privacy are we willing to give up in exchange for security?

The issue of security versus privacy goes far beyond terrorism. It arises in malls and parks where security cameras catch every action. It reaches into homes where parents bug their kids' rooms, into schools where students and administrators clash over drug tests, and into workplaces where bosses monitor employees' Internet use and read their e-mails. Anyone who has suffered identity theft or who worries about confidential medical information becoming public has confronted the problem of safeguarding privacy.

Clashes between security and privacy, however, often center on questions of national policy, which includes decisions about how best to protect the country. And the debate often stretches beyond the topic of purely personal privacy into the area of civil liberties, such as freedom of speech and freedom from unreasonable searches. That's because the modern notion of privacy that most Americans share today evolved along with the concept of civil liberties and civil rights. Many of our laws and practices concerning privacy stem from the Constitution's protections of civil liberties, as well as the many legal decisions that have interpreted how these constitutional guarantees apply to individual freedom.

National identity cards, airport searches of travelers who are not under suspicion, government surveillance of citizens, and the use of encryption software to keep Internet communications secret—all of these issues demand a balance between safety and security on one hand and privacy and liberty on the other. All of them were being debated before 9/11, but the events of that tragic September morning brought them to the center of public attention.

September 11, 2001

The aircraft that hit the WTC's north tower struck the 110-floor building near the top, between the ninety-third and ninety-eighth floors. Loaded with 15,000 gallons of jet fuel, the plane exploded into a fireball. The force of the impact and the explosion equaled that of nearly half a million pounds of TNT.

George Sleigh was talking on the phone in his office on the ninety-first floor when the jet hit. The ceiling fell on him, and the walls around him crumbled. Sleigh worked his way out from under the debris, and then he and ten coworkers made their way down one of the building's stairwells. It took them almost an hour to reach the ground level and get out of the building. They found the streets filled with rescue workers, ambulances, police cars, and fire trucks. Shocked and injured survivors were still staggering out of the building. To the horror of helpless onlookers, people on high floors of the tower, trapped by the blaze, were falling or leaping to their deaths. As the battered Sleigh was helped into an ambulance, he heard a police officer cry out, "The building is coming down!"

The building that fell at that moment wasn't the north tower of the WTC, where Sleigh had worked. It was the neighboring south tower, which had been hit by the second jet. Sleigh and his coworkers, like the great majority of people who were below the impact zone, survived because they were able to get out of the tower, but many of the survivors got out just in time. Both buildings, their structures weakened by the heat of the burning jet fuel, collapsed completely, killing about four hundred firefighters and police officers who had rushed to the scene to provide aid.

By the time the WTC towers fell, the nation knew that the crashes had not been accidents. They were attacks, and New York was not the only target. A third jet had flown into the Pentagon. A fourth plane, possibly also headed toward the nation's capital, had crashed in a field in Pennsylvania. Everyone aboard all four planes died, including the hijackers who had set the aircraft on their paths to destruction.

Across America and around the world, people heard the news and watched the horrifying events unfold on television screens. Cell phones brought startling and heartbreaking immediacy to the disaster. People who could not get out of the burning buildings talked to their loved ones, or left messages for them, before they died. *ABC News* broadcast a call from Jim Gartenberg, who was trapped on the eighty-sixth floor of the north WTC tower; he gave a live description of conditions there just before he perished in the building's collapse. The passengers of United Flight 93, the plane that slammed into the Pennsylvania countryside, learned about the other attacks through cellphone conversations. They then apparently fought back against their hijackers, causing the plane to crash.

As Manhattan surged with people fleeing the southern end of the island on foot, authorities declared states of emergency in New York City and Washington, D.C. The U.S. military was put on alert status everywhere in the world. Fearing that more attacks were on the way, federal officials evacuated the White House and Congress and ordered that no planes could take off from U.S. airports until further notice. Tens of thousands of confused and frightened travelers remained stranded in airports.

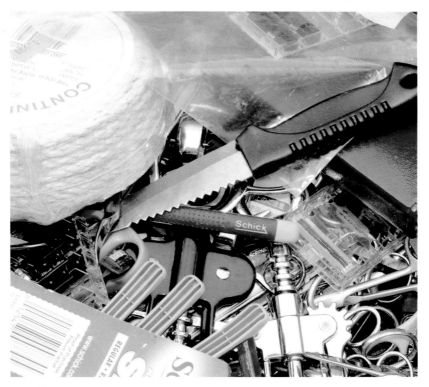

KNIVES, SCISSORS, AND A CORKSCREW WERE AMONG THE MORE
THAN TEN THOUSAND ITEMS CONFISCATED FROM TRAVELERS' CARRY-
ON BAGS AT LOS ANGELES INTERNATIONAL AIRPORT IN JUST TWO
DAYS WHEN AIR TRAVEL RESUMED AFTER 9/11. SUCH OBJECTS
WERE BANNED BECAUSE THE 9/11 HIJACKERS HAD USED BOXCUT-
TERS, OR UTILITY KNIVES, TO SEIZE CONTROL OF THE JETS.

Americans were stunned. Early estimates of the death
toll ranged as high as six or seven thousand. In the end, the
figure would prove to be far lower, though still dreadful.
The exact figure may never be known. No physical remains were found for many of those lost, and conflicting
reports and fraudulent claims further obscured the total.
Eventually, authorities confirmed 2,973 deaths in the September 11 attacks.

The attack left other wounds. In lower Manhattan, where the tallest towers in the land once stood, was a huge, smoldering pit filled with rubble that would take months to clear. Other buildings around the towers were crushed by their fall, or would later have to be destroyed because of structural damage. Businesses in the area suffered; some had to close for good. A sickening smell hung over the city like a noxious cloud, created by the tons of pollutants released into the air by the crashes and the collapse of the buildings. The long-term environmental and health damage is not yet fully known.

The deepest wound may have been to Americans' sense of security. Everyday activities—going to work, boarding a plane—had suddenly turned horrific. A swift and savage blow had been dealt to the country's biggest city and to its capital. From the highest levels of government to the families who gathered in front of their television sets, watching the smoke plumes rise over New York and Washington, D.C., people asked how such a thing could have happened, and how it could be prevented from happening again.

The Terrorist Threat

Within minutes of the attacks, government bodies such as the Central Intelligence Agency (CIA), the Federal Bureau of Investigation (FBI), and the Federal Aviation Administration (FAA) launched an investigation to discover what had happened. On September 14, the government published the names of nineteen men—from Saudi Arabia, the United Arab Emirates, Egypt, and Lebanon—who had boarded the four flights as passengers, then used boxcutters or other small knives to overpower the crew and take control of the planes.

Some of the suspected hijackers had been in the United

States for several years. Others had just arrived. A few of them had enrolled in flight schools to learn how to handle aircraft, or had sought information about crop-dusting planes, which authorities feared might be part of a plan to spread biological or chemical weapons. All nineteen of the hijackers were believed to have ties to an international terrorist network known as Al-Qaeda.

Government and intelligence officials in the United States and some other countries consider Al-Qaeda responsible for the 9/11 attacks, as well as for terrorist incidents before and after that day. Led by an Islamic radical named Osama bin Laden, Al-Qaeda had already demonstrated its hostility to the United States, as well as its willingness to use terrorist tactics, such as attacks on civilians, against those countries it saw as its enemies. In 1998, for example, Al-Qaeda had organized bombings at two U.S. embassies in Africa that killed more than two hundred people. Many U.S. intelligence experts think that Al-Qaeda was also responsible for a 2000 attack on the U.S.S. *Cole*, a Navy ship that was in the port of Aden, in Yemen, by suicide bombers in a small boat.

Why would Al-Qaeda attack the United States? Many explanations have been offered for the group's anger toward America—an anger shared by other Islamic individuals and organizations that are usually described as radicals or extremists. Al-Qaeda itself has stated that it opposes specific actions by the United States. One of these actions is supporting the Middle Eastern state of Israel, which Al-Qaeda equates with oppressing Arab Palestinians in the region. Another is maintaining military bases in Saudi Arabia, the birthplace of Islam. A third is interfering with the politics and economies of Islamic nations. Some observers of Al-Qaeda and other Islamic extremists believe that these groups' opposition is more general, based on a hatred of Western culture and a desire to overthrow

"Freedom and Fear Are at War": The President Speaks

On September 20, 2001, nine days after the attacks on New York City and Washington, D.C., President George W. Bush spoke to the U.S. Congress and the American people. Calling upon Americans to remain steadfastly devoted to the principles of their democratic government, Bush talked about the enemy who had struck the deadly blows on 9/11. The radical Islamists of Al-Qaeda, he declared, had something in common with the Fascists, Nazis, and others who had used force to create totalitarian regimes in the twentieth century. They were willing to sacrifice innocent lives in the service of their beliefs—and were unwilling to tolerate the beliefs of others.

Bush emphasized the country's determination to fight back against terrorism. He outlined the steps that the United States would take to stamp out terrorists and their supporters at home and around the world. Interrupted by bursts of applause from members of Congress, Bush told his audience in the Capitol and across the nation:

> . . . **On September the 11th, enemies of freedom committed an act of war against our country. Americans have known wars, but for the past 136 years they have been wars on foreign soil, except for one Sunday in 1941. [Bush was referring to the Japanese attack on Pearl Harbor that brought**

the United States into World War II.] Americans have known the casualties of war, but not at the center of a great city on a peaceful morning.

Americans have known surprise attacks, but never before on thousands of civilians. All of this was brought upon us in a single day, and night fell on a different world, a world where freedom itself is under attack. . . .

Al Qaeda is to terror what the Mafia is to crime. But its goal is not making money, its goal is remaking the world and imposing its radical beliefs on people everywhere. . . .

They hate what they see right here in this chamber: a democratically elected government. Their leaders are self-appointed. They hate our freedoms: our freedom of religion, our freedom of speech, our freedom to vote and assemble and disagree with each other. . . .

We will direct every resource at our command—every means of diplomacy, every tool of intelligence, every instrument of law enforcement, every financial influence, and every necessary weapon of war—to the destruction and to the defeat of the global terror network. . . .

From this day forward, any nation that continues to harbor or support terrorism will be regarded by the United States as a hostile regime. Our nation has been put on notice: We're not immune from attack. We will take defensive measures against terrorism to protect Americans. . . .

This is not, however, just America's fight. And what is at stake is not just America's freedom. This is the world's fight. This is civilization's fight. This is the fight of all who believe in progress and pluralism, tolerance and freedom. . . .

As long as the United States of America is determined and strong, this will not be an age of terror. This will be an age of liberty here and across the world. . . .

Freedom and fear are at war. The advance of human freedom, the great achievement of our time and the great hope of every time, now depends on us. . . .

democracy and freedom. This view was shared by President George W. Bush, who commanded the U.S. response to the 9/11 attacks.

Whatever Al-Qaeda's motives, Americans across the political spectrum agreed that terrorist attacks could not be tolerated. In the wake of the 9/11 disaster, as citizens expressed themselves with an outburst of flags and patriotic stickers—and with an outpouring of charity toward the families of the victims—the government launched a series of coordinated, far-reaching actions to combat terrorism. Collectively called the "War on Terror" by the Bush administration, these actions took effect in other nations, at the U.S. border, and also in the domestic sphere, within the United States.

One immediate action concerned money. Using powers granted under a 1977 law called the International Emergency Economic Powers Act, President Bush signed an executive order that froze the assets of Osama Bin Laden, Al-Qaeda, and other people and organizations that the CIA or the FBI suspected of having ties to terrorist groups. This prevented them from moving money out of accounts or using credit cards.

In the days after 9/11 it became sadly clear that poor communication within and among U.S. intelligence and law enforcement organizations had caused warnings about possible terrorist activities to be overlooked. In the hope of preventing such blunders in the future, soon after the attacks the president created a new federal agency called the Office of Homeland Security. Its role was to coordinate antiterrorist activities in the United States. In November 2002 the agency was upgraded to the Department of Homeland Security (DHS), and the Cabinet—the group of nonelected administrators who head key federal agencies and advise the president—was expanded to include the secretary of the DHS.

The domestic antiterror campaign, the government argued, required new or increased powers for intelligence and law enforcement organizations. They needed to be able to act faster and more comprehensively to gather information, to place suspects under surveillance (including monitoring their telephone and Internet communications), to detain and deport illegal aliens, and to seize the property of terrorist organizations. On September 24, 2001, United States Attorney General John Ashcroft spoke to a committee in the House of Representatives, urging Congress to pass laws to strengthen the government's antiterrorism powers. Ashcroft said:

> **This new terrorist threat to Americans on our soil is a turning point in American history. It's a new challenge for law enforcement. Our fight against terrorism is not merely or primarily a criminal justice endeavor. It is [a] defense of our nation and its citizens. We cannot wait for terrorists to strike to begin investigations and to take action. The death tolls are too high, the consequences too great. We must prevent first—we must prosecute second.**
>
> **The fight against terrorism is now the highest priority of the Department of Justice. As we do in each and every law enforcement mission we undertake, we are conducting this effort with a total commitment to protect the rights and privacy of all Americans and the constitutional protections we hold dear.**

The Department of Homeland Security was the first federal agency required by law to include a Privacy Office. The DHS describes the purpose of this office as "to minimize the impact on the individual's privacy, particularly

PROTESTORS DEMONSTRATE AGAINST THE **USA PATRIOT** ACT,
PASSED IN **2001** TO GIVE THE GOVERNMENT NEW POWERS TO
COMBAT TERRORISM. **MANY** PEOPLE CRITICIZED THE ACT FOR
INTRUDING TOO FAR ON PRIVACY AND CIVIL LIBERTIES.

the individual's personal information and dignity, while
achieving the mission of the Department of Homeland Security." Yet in the months and years to come, the government's antiterrorism policies and practices would cause
alarm among people who feared that the government
was violating both personal privacy and civil rights in the
name of security. Their fears were expressed by Aryeh

Neier, a journalist and former executive director of the organization Human Rights Watch, who wrote in 2003, "Major new violations of rights have already become a part of American law and practice. We are at risk of entering another of those dark periods of American history when the country abandons its proud tradition of respect for civil liberties."

Many Americans, however, were more worried about terrorist attacks than about potential violations of privacy and civil liberties. They felt that protecting the nation and its people must come first, and that anything that might protect the nation from another terrorist attack should be done. Commentator Heather MacDonald expressed this view when she wrote in *City Journal*, also in 2003,

> **Nothing the Bush administration has done comes close to causing the loss of freedom that Americans experienced after 9/11, when air travel shut down for days, and fear kept hundreds of thousands shut up in their homes. Should [Al-Qaeda] strike again, fear will once again paralyze the country far beyond the effects of any possible government restriction on civil rights. And that is what the government is trying to forestall, in the knowledge that preserving security is essential to preserving freedom.**

After 9/11, U.S. border security came under intense scrutiny as authorities learned that some of the hijackers had entered the United States on student visas that were long expired. Amid demands for closer monitoring of foreign nationals in the United States, the Immigration and Naturalization Service (INS) was merged into the new DHS in January 2003. Attention turned to U.S. ports, which some observers considered highly vulnerable to terrorist attacks. Another risk related to port security was the possibility that terrorists or explosives could be smuggled into the country in cargo containers. The issue of illegal border crossings from Mexico took on new urgency as concern mounted that terrorists might enter the country by the routes long used by undocumented immigrants.

Abroad, the United States struck quickly at what the administration considered to be the root of the 9/11 attacks. The first target was Afghanistan. Al-Qaeda operatives, most likely including Bin Laden, were known to maintain camps in this western Asian nation under the protection of the Taliban, the conservative Islamic party that controlled the country. The United States demanded that Afghanistan close the camps and turn over bin Laden and other Al-Qaeda members to U.S. authorities. The Taliban refused this demand. On October 7, 2001, the United States began dropping bombs on Afghanistan, focusing on suspected Al-Qaeda training camps and Taliban military sites. In 2003 the scope of U.S. military activity in the region would widen to include a war in the neighboring nation of Iraq, under the claim—later shown to be wrong—that Iraqi dictator Saddam Hussein and his government were directly linked to Al-Qaeda and the events of 9/11.

Even before the first bombs fell on Afghanistan, many Americans, both public figures and ordinary citizens, realized that 9/11 would change life at home, too. During past times of war and crisis, the government had taken strong measures—even drastic ones—aimed at ensuring public order and safety. Perhaps such measures were again necessary. Less than three weeks after the 9/11 attacks, Supreme Court Justice Sandra Day O'Connor said, "We're likely to experience more restrictions on our personal freedom than has ever been the case in our country. . . . [9/11] will cause us to re-examine some of our laws pertaining to criminal surveillance, wiretapping, immigration, and so on."

O'Connor spoke those words to a group of law students after making an emotional visit to the ruins of the World Trade Center. She rightly foresaw that one vital task facing the nation in the aftermath of 9/11 was reassessing the balance of security and privacy. By that time, members of the U.S. government were already at work crafting a new law designed to promote the war on terror within the United States. Known as the USA PATRIOT Act (which stands for the Uniting and Strengthening America by Providing Appropriate Tools Required to Intercept and Obstruct Terrorism Act), that law would become part of a legal and social debate about freedom, security, and privacy that had started before the founding of the United States.

2
Privacy and the Law

What if the government had cameras and microphones everywhere, not just in public places, but in every home and apartment? What if everyone were trained to view everyone else with suspicion—neighbors urged to report each other's doings to the authorities, children encouraged to spy and report on their parents? What if Thought Police tortured people not just for doing wrong, but for saying forbidden things, even for having forbidden thoughts?

British writer George Orwell depicted this nightmarish world in his 1949 novel *1984*. In Orwell's fictional realm of Oceania, an all-powerful totalitarian government known as Big Brother has replaced truth with lies, history with propaganda, and civil liberties with perpetual surveillance. *1984* is a dystopia, a type of fiction that conjures up the worst possible worlds. Orwell's dark vision is frightening not just because it paints a picture of endless war and loveless life, but because it portrays a state that has stripped its citizens of their privacy, which many people regard as essential to dignity and humanity. Most, however,

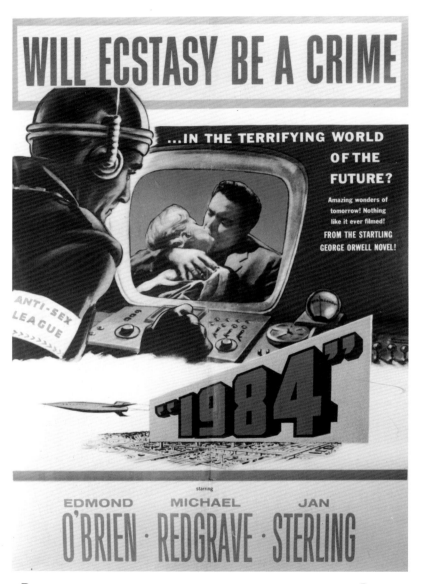

PRIVACY IS A THING OF THE PAST IN THE NIGHTMARISH WORLD OF GEORGE ORWELL'S NOVEL *1984*. A POSTER FOR THE 1956 MOVIE SHOWS A MEMBER OF THE ANTI-SEX LEAGUE USING A TELEVISION MONITOR TO SPY ON A COUPLE DURING WHAT THEY THINK IS A SECRET TRYST.

would probably agree that the privacy of individuals must be balanced with the common good of society. The difficulty, of course, is finding and maintaining a good balance.

Do you consider privacy a constitutional right in the United States? If so, you are not alone. In 1999, a Gallup poll revealed that 70 percent of Americans believed that the right to privacy is guaranteed by the U.S. Constitution. They were wrong. The word *privacy* appears nowhere in the Constitution. Although privacy is legally protected in the United States, the protections evolved over time in a series of court decisions. Privacy, in fact, turns out to be a somewhat vague and slippery notion under the law.

Civil Liberties

The rights and freedoms that people possess as members of a society are often grouped together under the label "civil liberties." Usually defined by laws or by a ruler or a government, civil liberties vary widely from country to country. The civil liberties enjoyed by citizens of the United States are, like much else in American law and government, based in part on an English model.

In 1689 the English Parliament passed a law that became known as a Bill of Rights. The law spelled out certain freedoms that citizens possessed, including freedom to petition the monarch, freedom to elect members of Parliament without interference from the monarch, freedom from cruel and unusual punishments, and freedom from being fined or from being deprived of property or privileges without a trial.

The intellectual movement known as the Enlightenment further developed the idea of civil liberties. Starting at the end of the seventeenth century and continuing through the eighteenth, Western historians, philosophers, scientists, and other thinkers contributed to this movement, which celebrated the power of reason. Through the use of reason, Enlightenment thinkers believed, people could dispel the darkness of superstition and tyranny, attain knowledge, and improve the human condition. Among the topics toward which they turned their critical gaze was government—specifically, the proper relationship between individuals and the state.

The notion of mutual rights and responsibilities was a cornerstone of much Enlightenment political thought. In this view, people empower their governments with certain rights, such as the right to collect taxes and the right to make war. The government also has responsibilities to the citizens. It must protect them, for example, and it must act according to law and not by the whim of a dictator or monarch. The citizens must meet their own responsibilities, such as paying taxes and obeying laws; in return, they have certain rights and privileges, such as those contained in the English Bill of Rights. The writers of the Enlightenment had a great variety of theories about the ideal state, but most of them felt that people are entitled to basic liberties and that it is the duty of the state, or the government, to guarantee and protect those liberties.

The major thinkers of the Enlightenment were French, English, and Scottish, but their ideas traveled across the Atlantic Ocean to Britain's American colonies. Works such as *Two Treatises on Government* (1689), by the English philosopher John Locke, shaped the thinking of Thomas Jefferson, Thomas Paine, and others who sought independence for the colonies. Once the colonies had gained their independence in the Revolutionary War, they had to create a framework for governing their new democratic republic. The result was the U.S. Constitution, shaped in part by the ideals of the Enlightenment and in part by a fierce tug-of-war between two opposing groups of the nation's founders, the Federalists and the Antifederalists. The tension that exists today between protecting individual privacy and preserving national security echoes the disagreement that arose in the late 1780s between these two groups.

The Federalists wanted a strong federal, or national, government. They feared that without a powerful central authority, the young United States would be overwhelmed by war, disorder, or revolts and uprisings among the people, several of which had already occurred. The Federalist position was shared by, among others, George Washington and James Madison, the country's first and fourth presidents. Antifederalists like Patrick Henry, on the other hand, wanted to see more power in the hands of local governments and less in the hands of a federal government. They feared that a strong central power could too easily become tyrannical, or could be dominated by the rich or by special interests. The Antifederalists' chief objection to the Constitution as it was originally written was that it did not guarantee civil liberties. Still, after being ratified by nine of the thirteen states, the Constitution went into effect in 1788.

Four years later, Congress added ten amendments to the Constitution to address the issue of civil liberties. Those ten amendments are usually referred to as the American Bill of Rights. They use some of the language of the English Bill of Rights—the Eighth Amendment, for example, which guarantees protection from cruel and unusual punishments, was copied word-for-word from the English bill.

Security and privacy questions often relate to the Fourth Amendment, which states,

The right of the people to be secure in their persons, houses, papers, and effects, against unreasonable searches and seizures, shall not be violated, and no Warrants shall issue, but upon

Enlightened
Disagreement

Benjamin Franklin—businessman, inventor, diplomat, Enlightenment thinker, and one of the founders of the United States—
is mentioned in many debates about civil liberties and public
security. People who fear that tightened security measures
threaten civil liberties often quote (or misquote) these words
attributed to Franklin:

> **Those who would give up essential liberty to pur-
> chase a little temporary safety, deserve neither
> liberty nor safety.**

Sacrificing vital freedoms, Franklin seems to say, is a terri-
ble way to achieve some small measure of safety. What is lost
is larger and more precious than anything that could possibly be
gained. A lot of people see this statement as evidence that the
much-respected Franklin would have done anything to preserve
civil rights rather than knuckle under to fear. Yet few are aware
of the statement's context.

The bold words about liberty and safety do not come from the era of the Revolutionary War, the struggle to establish American freedom, or the writing of the U.S. Constitution. They date from two decades earlier in the colonial period. The quoted sentence first appeared in print in *An Historical Review of the Constitution and Government of Pennsylvania*, which went to press in 1759 in London, while Franklin was living in England. Although published anonymously, the work was quickly associated with Franklin. The sentence was copied from a letter that the Pennsylvania Assembly had sent to the colony's governor in 1755. Both the letter and the *Historical Review* dealt with lengthy disputes between the settlers in Pennsylvania and the colony's owners, the family of William Penn.

Soon after the *Historical Review* was published, Franklin wrote to a friend named David Hume, a Scottish historian and philosopher who was one of the leading philosophers of the Enlightenment. Hume had congratulated Franklin on the *Historical Review*, but Franklin replied that he had written only parts of it, including some of the Assembly's letters and documents that were quoted. It's impossible to say for certain that Franklin is the author of the "liberty for safety" quote, although scholars who have studied his work agree that it sounds like him.

Hume had touched on a related subject a few years earlier, in a book titled *Enquiry Concerning the Principles of Morals* (1751). In a discussion of justice, Hume argued that in a time of war a nation might have to suspend justice:

The rage and violence of public war; what is it but a suspension of justice among the warring parties, who perceive, that this virtue is now no longer of any *use* or advantage to them? The laws of war, which then succeed to those of equity and justice, are rules calculated for the *advantage* and *utility* of that particular state, in which men are now placed. And were a civilized nation engaged with barbarians, who observed no rules even of war, the

former must also suspend their observance of them, where they no longer serve to any purpose; and must render every action or recounter as bloody and pernicious as possible to the first aggressors.

Do whatever it takes to win, Hume seems to be saying. If a civilized nation finds itself at war with people who do not follow the rules of combat, then the civilized nation must depart from the rules, too. Hume was writing about how a nation at war deals with outside enemies. Could his argument that the needs of war override the principles of justice apply also to a nation's treatment of its own citizens?

Two Enlightenment philosophers—and two different views of the right balance between liberty and safety, between the rule of law and the rules of war. For the United States in the aftermath of 9/11, finding that balance has become a challenge.

probable cause, supported by Oath or affirmation, and particularly describing the place to be searched, and the persons or things to be seized.

This amendment was, at least in part, a reaction to the former British practice of using documents called writs of assistance. These writs functioned like search warrants, except that they were general, or universal. An official in possession of such a writ could search anyone or anything, or seize private property, without having to say what crime the subject of the search was suspected of committing. Abuse of writs sometimes resulted in intimidation, harassment, or outright theft.

The Fourth Amendment established that freedom from such arbitrary arrests is a constitutionally protected civil liberty. The amendment reflects the view that the government cannot inquire into what you do, enter your home, or examine your papers and other possessions unless it gives reasons for believing that you have broken the law, and specifies what evidence it hopes to find. Although the amendment does not contain the word privacy, it clearly expresses the concept.

The Fourteenth Amendment, which was added to the Constitution in 1868, approaches the issues of privacy and security from a different direction. This amendment reads,

No State shall make or enforce any law which shall abridge the privileges or immunities of citizens of the United States; nor shall any state deprive any person of life, liberty, or property, without due process of law, nor deny to any person within its jurisdiction the equal protection of the laws.

The Fourteenth Amendment guarantees lawful and equal treatment for all. Like the Fourth Amendment's protection from unreasonable search and seizure, this guarantee later became a basis for court decisions on matters of privacy versus law enforcement or security.

"The Right to Privacy"

Privacy has meant different things in different cultures and eras. The ancient Greek philosopher Aristotle, for example, wrote about two realms of human activity. One realm was public life, which had to do with politics and the activities of the state or community. The other was private life. To Aristotle, private life meant the domestic life of the family or household, which was dominated by the husband and father. This head of the household would have considered that what took place under his roof was his private business and was of no concern to the larger world—but he would most likely not have considered that his wife, children, servants, or slaves had a right to their own privacy.

Modern Western ideas about privacy were strongly influenced by Enlightenment writings on individual rights and by the passage of legal or constitutional guarantees of civil liberties. Privacy came to be highly valued in many modern societies, especially in Western industrialized countries that place a high value on individualism, such as the United States.

In 1890 two American law partners named Samuel Warren and Louis Brandeis wrote an article titled "The Right to Privacy" for the *Harvard Law Review*. Their essay was a milestone because it raised, for the first time, the question of what privacy meant in terms of U.S. law. (Brandeis would later serve as a justice on the U.S. Supreme Court, from 1916 to 1939.)

In considering privacy and the law, Warren and Brandeis were venturing into new territory. Unlike criminal law and many areas of civil law, privacy did not have a legal

FIFTEEN CENTS   November 15, 1937

TIME

The Weekly Newsmagazine

Volume XXX

MR. JUSTICE LOUIS DEMBITZ BRANDEIS
"Care is taken that the trees do not scrape the skies."
(See NATIONAL AFFAIRS)

Number 20

BEFORE HE BECAME A JUSTICE OF THE U.S. SUPREME COURT, ATTORNEY LOUIS D. BRANDEIS WAS ONE OF THE AUTHORS OF AN INFLUENTIAL ESSAY CALLED "THE RIGHT TO PRIVACY," WHICH SHAPED THE DEVELOPMENT OF PRIVACY LAWS IN THE UNITED STATES.

Privacy and Technology

When they wrote their influential 1890 article "The Right to Privacy," Samuel Warren and Louis Brandeis were especially worried about the way personal privacy was being redefined by a new invention: the snapshot camera, created by American George Eastman and introduced to the public in 1888.

Before the snapshot camera, taking a photograph was a somewhat complicated procedure. The photographer had to load a camera with a chemical-coated glass plate to record the image. It wasn't impossible to take a photograph furtively, or in secret. Some cameras had been made in the shape of hats, canes, and other common objects so that photographers could take pictures without anyone knowing they were doing it, but such cameras were not easy to use, and they were costly. The snapshot camera, marketed under the name Kodak, replaced the bulky glass plate with a roll of film mounted on lightweight paper or celluloid. The Kodak was affordable, easy to carry, and a snap to use. Suddenly anyone could be a photographer, taking instant images of anything and anyone.

People quickly found uses for this new technology, and just as quickly, other people disapproved. They feared that the camera—and another new invention, the voice recorder—could intrude on privacy and violate the standards of decent behavior. In "The Right to Privacy," Warren and Brandeis identified twin threats to personal and domestic privacy: the snapshot camera and the media. They wrote, "Instantaneous photographs and newspaper enterprise have invaded the sacred precincts of private and domestic life; and numerous mechanical devices threaten to make good the prediction that 'what is whispered in the closet shall be proclaimed from the house-tops.'"

Warren and Brandeis were not alone in having trouble adjusting to the ways people were using new tools such as the Kodak camera. In 1893 a writer for a British newspaper called the *Weekly Times and Echo* announced, "Several decent young men, I hear, are forming a Vigilance Association for the purpose of thrashing the cads with cameras who go about at seaside places taking snapshots at ladies emerging from the deep in the mournful garments peculiar to the British female bather." Although anyone on a public beach could look at girls in their droopy suits of wet wool, this newspaper writer and the "decent young men" felt that it was wrong, somehow, to photograph them.

The technology has been updated, but the questions that troubled Warren and Brandeis remain. Millions of people now carry cell phones that can take photographs; many phones also record video clips. That girl on the bus with her phone to her ear—could she be taking a picture of you? Did someone film you as you tripped over the curb outside school today and sent your books flying? What if someone uploads a photo or video of you to a Web site without your knowledge, or uses it in a work of art? Have your rights been violated?

Cell phones are everywhere, and they seem innocent. These inconspicuous handheld cameras have been used for unsavory or illegal purposes, such as snapping "upskirt" pictures of women on escalators or secretly photographing people in dressing rooms. Yet quick-thinking bystanders have also used their cell phone cameras to foil crimes and help police track down criminals. Stealth photography has become a fact of modern life. Like other technologies that have emerged over the years—and those that will undoubtedly emerge in the future— the easy-to-use camera has forced us to think again about privacy, and about how we define it.

history. No ancient or medieval law codes included privacy statutes. The subject had not been addressed in court cases that could serve as legal precedents. Nor was privacy specifically recognized as a constitutional right. Warren and Brandeis were, essentially, inventing the legal and constitutional grounds for recognizing privacy as something to be protected.

Warren and Brandeis pointed out that the law had long acknowledged people's right to be protected in their person and their property. This meant that the law recognized individuals' rights to personal liberty, or freedom from physical restraint; their control over who entered their homes; and their ownership of their ideas and thoughts as expressed in writing. "Gradually the scope of these legal rights [has] broadened," wrote Warren and Brandeis, "and now the right to life has come to mean the right to enjoy life,—the right to be let alone; the right to liberty secures the exercise of extensive civil privileges; and the term 'property' has grown to comprise every form of possession—intangible, as well as tangible."

The phrase "the right to be let alone" sums up the idea of privacy as freedom from invasion or intrusion. Warren and Brandeis were especially concerned with a particular kind of intrusion: the unauthorized publication of information and photographs. They argued for legal recognition of something they called "the right to one's personality." That right would include control over information about oneself and images of oneself. The unauthorized possession or use of such information or images would be an invasion of privacy. The two authors realized that there must be exceptions. Someone running for public office, for example, was a legitimate subject of interest. Information about such a candidate could be freely published, as long as it did not break the laws that already existed to protect people from slander and libel, statements about someone that are false or that unjustly present the person in an unfavorable way.

"The Right to Privacy" was widely read and enormously influential. It became the basis for many of the civil laws that are designed to protect people's privacy and punish violations. (Civil laws apply to interactions among individuals that are the subject of private lawsuits, not of criminal charges.)

In the Zone

Civil law is one aspect of the modern American notion of privacy. Another aspect is constitutional law. Privacy in this legal context has been shaped largely by how the U.S. Supreme Court, the nation's highest court, has applied or interpreted certain parts of the Constitution over the years.

One of the Court's early and important privacy decisions came in 1891, when the Supreme Court heard the case of *Union Pacific Railway* v. *Botsford*. This case involved a railway employee named Clara Botsford who sued the company over an injury that occurred on a train. The railway would not pay damages unless Botsford agreed to a doctor's examination that would require her to undress. Botsford refused, arguing that being seen without clothing would violate her privacy. A lower court supported Botsford. The railway company appealed the decision to the Supreme Court. The Court ruled in Botsford's favor, basing its decision on the Fourth Amendment's protection against unreasonable search and seizure. The Court held that an individual's right to control his or her own person (body) must be safeguarded by the law.

A landmark case in 1965 led the Supreme Court to issue its first ruling that dealt directly and specifically with privacy. *Griswold* v. *Connecticut* concerned a doctor at Yale Medical School and a director of Planned Parenthood who had been convicted under a Connecticut state law that made it illegal to provide information about birth control, even to married couples. The Supreme Court overturned their convictions and ruled that the Connecticut law was unconstitutional. Pointing to the Ninth Amendment, which states that the rights of the people are not limited to the rights that are specifically granted in the Constitution, the Court ruled that couples have the right to privacy concerning marital matters, including reproduction. Justice William O. Douglas, who wrote the Court's majority opinion in the *Griswold* case, said that the Constitution's amendments allow people to create "zones of privacy."

Griswold equated privacy with autonomy, or self-determination and independence, in making personal and family decisions without the interference of the state. The zone of privacy surrounding those decisions has expanded and contracted over the years because the way the Supreme Court defines and defends the zone depends upon the makeup of the Court at any given time. In 1973 the Court widened the zone in *Roe* v. *Wade*, a case that overturned a Texas law and granted women the right to have legal abortions. Thirteen years later, however, the Court defined the zone of privacy more narrowly in the case of *Bowers* v. *Hardwick*, ruling that the claim of privacy could not be used to overturn a Georgia law against certain kinds of sexual behavior. In 2003, however, the Court's decision in *Lawrence* v. *Texas* reversed the *Bowers* decision. In *Lawrence*, the Court ruled that the state could not outlaw the behavior in question between consenting adults.

The Supreme Court addressed another kind of privacy in the 1967 case *Katz* v. *United States*. Charles Katz was convicted of illegal gambling in California based on recordings of telephone calls that he had made to place his bets. Katz had used a pay phone in a public phone booth, not knowing that the FBI had bugged the phone in the hope of obtaining evidence against him; the FBI, however, had not gotten a warrant authorizing it to tap the phone. Katz appealed his conviction on the grounds that the recordings had been obtained illegally. An appeals court upheld the conviction. It declared that the FBI's use of wiretapping equipment was not the same thing as a physical invasion of the phone booth, and therefore it did not require a warrant. Katz appealed the case to the Supreme Court. The Court decided in Katz's favor, finding the warrantless wiretap unconstitutional. Because it was reasonable for Katz to expect that his telephone conversations would remain private, said the Court, the FBI needed a warrant to intrude upon them. The *Katz* case established the principle that violating someone's "reasonable expectation of privacy" without a show of "probable cause" and a warrant is prohibited by the Fourth Amendment.

Privacy Law Today

Precious though it is, privacy is hard to pin down. Instead of having a single, constitutional definition, privacy has been defined by a complex set of laws and court decisions. Some legal scholars recognize multiple kinds of privacy, such as physical privacy (freedom from intrusion), informational privacy (the right to control personal information and images), and decisional privacy or autonomy (the right to make personal decisions). Others argue that "privacy" as a distinct right or legal concept is meaningless because it is so ill-defined and because its various aspects are governed separately by different laws.

The body of civil law that protects the privacy of the individual falls into four categories that were defined by legal scholar William Dean Prosser in "Privacy," a 1960 article in the *California Law Review*. The four categories are intrusion, appropriation, publication of private facts, and false light. Although privacy laws vary from state to state, and although the laws are constantly being modified to keep pace with developments in society and technology (such as the rise of professional paparazzi who snap photos of celebrities, or the widespread use of personal computers), the four categories still form the framework for most civil lawsuits connected with privacy invasion. Some of the actions in these categories are also subject to criminal penalties.

Intrusion means breaking into private areas, either by trespassing, by wiretapping or some other form of surveillance, or by electronic means, such as hacking into Web sites, databases, or computers. *Appropriation* is the use of someone's name, image, or words for commercial purposes, as in advertising, without the person's consent. The *publication of private facts* is just that—the release of information that is personal, confidential, or not a legitimate subject of public interest. (For information to be protected, however, it must be truly private and not available in public records.) *False light* means publishing information that portrays someone in an offensive, negative, erroneous, or embarrassing way. All of these categories are subject to a wide range of interpretation by the courts.

When privacy clashes with security, the issues are often constitutional matters of "search and seizure" or "due process of law," rather than matters of civil law. A population, government, or Supreme Court that favors strong protections for privacy may find itself shifting its position in time of war or crisis, when it may lean more toward public safety and security. After the 9/11 terrorist attacks, Americans were called upon to consider the limits of both security and privacy when the U.S. government took aim at terrorism with the sweeping new Patriot Act.

3
Patriotic Protection or Loss of Civil Liberties?

One week after the 9/11 attacks on New York City and Washington, D.C., some envelopes passed through a postal facility in Trenton, New Jersey. They were post-marked and sent on their way to the media organizations—television news programs and newspaper publishers—to which they were addressed. Inside the envelopes were notes that mentioned 9/11 and contained the phrases "This is next" and "Death to America."

The envelopes held more than menacing notes. They also contained spores of the anthrax bacterium, which causes potentially fatal disease in humans and some animals. Five such letters had been mailed, possibly from Princeton, New Jersey, although only two were later recovered. Three weeks later, anthrax-contaminated notes were sent to two Democratic U.S. senators, Tom Daschle of South Dakota, the Senate minority leader, and Patrick Leahy of Vermont.

SORTING MAIL BECAME POTENTIALLY LIFE-THREATENING DURING THE ANTHRAX SCARE OF 2001. IN THE WEEKS AFTER 9/11, LETTERS CONTAMINATED WITH THE DEADLY DISEASE KILLED FIVE PEOPLE AND FUELED AMERICANS' FEARS OF COMING UNDER ASSAULT FROM MANY DIFFERENT DIRECTIONS.

At first, no one realized that the powdery material in the envelopes was anthrax. When people who had handled the envelopes or notes started to get sick, they were diagnosed with other conditions, such as pneumonia. On October 4, however, a victim of the first mailing was publicly confirmed to have inhalation anthrax, the most severe form of the disease. His was the first known case of anthrax in the United States since 1976. He died the following day. In all, five people died and seventeen got sick as a result of the anthrax letters sent in the fall of 2001. As of early 2007, the FBI investigation of the case remained open; the person or persons responsible for the mailings had not been identified.

As it became clear that anthrax was being deliberately transmitted as a terrorist tactic, panic spread. People wondered whether biological warfare would escalate. There were fears that large-scale contamination of buildings' ventilation systems or of communities' water systems could spread disease to thousands of people, possibly infecting whole cities.

Fortunately, the anthrax scare did not turn into a large-scale biological terror attack. As far as is known, there were no more anthrax letters and no further incidents of biological terrorism in the United States. Yet at the time—with the remains of 9/11 victims still being recovered from the World Trade Center ruins—the anthrax mailings fueled people's fears that the country was under attack from multiple sources, by multiple methods. In this climate of anxiety and anger, the nation's legislators passed a law that had been hurriedly written in response to the threat of terrorism. The new law gave the government some powers that it desperately wanted in order to wage a coordinated war on terror, yet it also raised concerns that civil liberties would be bent or broken in the name of security.

The USA PATRIOT Act

The USA PATRIOT Act, or simply the Patriot Act, as previously mentioned, was passed in response to the terror of 9/11. Its principal authors were Viet Dinh, an assistant attorney general, and Michael Chertoff, who was head of criminal justice at the Department of Justice at the time; in 2005 he would be named secretary of Homeland Security. The Patriot Act was introduced as a bill into the House of

Representatives on October 23, 2001, by Congressman James Sensenbrenner of Wisconsin. The next day, the House passed it in a vote of 357 to 66. The day after that, the bill went to the Senate, where ninety-eight senators voted to pass it. Russ Feingold of Wisconsin voted against the bill, and Mary Landrieu of Louisiana did not vote.

On October 26 President Bush signed the bill into law, and the Patriot Act went into effect. It expanded governmental powers that had been set by a number of earlier laws. One of these laws was the Foreign Intelligence Surveillance Act (FISA) of 1978. FISA had authorized the creation of secret panels of judges to oversee wiretap requests and other matters during investigations of foreigners or of Americans who were suspected of being covert foreign agents. FISA was aimed at suspected spies or terrorists operating within the United States. It let law enforcement agencies get the warrants needed to investigate such suspects quickly and with high security. FISA warrants' standards of protection for the individual were significantly lower than those of the ordinary warrants that law enforcement agencies had to use when investigating domestic cases, which do not involve foreign people or countries. Agents applying for FISA warrants, for example, did not have to give the probable cause for suspicion, the reasoning or evidence that explains why the suspect should be investigated. Requests for FISA warrants were almost never turned down. Some 15,000 FISA warrants were issued between 1978 and 2002; during that same period, one percent of requests were rejected.

The Patriot Act established the category of domestic terrorism and extended FISA standards to cover investigations in that category. This expanded the power of federal agencies and law enforcement bodies to conduct secret wiretaps and searches and to collect information about people—such as academic records, library records, and

44

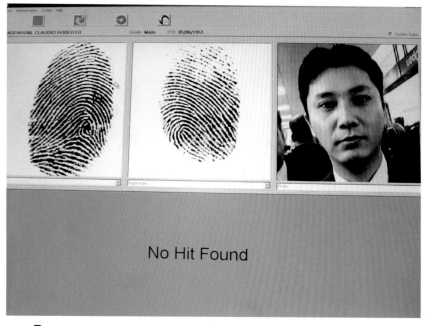

No Hit Found

BIOMETRIC DATA—INKLESS FINGERPRINTS AND DIGITAL PHOTO-
GRAPHS—ARE COLLECTED AS FOREIGNERS ENTER THE COUNTRY UNDER
THE UNITED STATES VISITOR AND IMMIGRANT STATUS INDICATOR
TECHNOLOGY PROGAM (US-VISIT). LAUNCHED IN 2004, THE PRO-
GRAM HELPS THE GOVERNMENT MONITOR FOREIGN NATIONALS WITHIN
THE UNITED STATES.

medical records—without the subjects' knowledge and
without providing a reason. The act also strengthened
criminal laws and penalties concerned with terrorism,
made it easier for authorities to track and seize the financial assets of people and organizations linked to terrorism,
and established benefits for victims of terrorism.

Before the Patriot Act, the CIA, the FBI, and the U.S.
Treasury Department were not permitted to share information, for fear that one agency might influence or interfere with another agency's operations, or that private

information might be misused or leaked to the press or the public. Another reason for separation among the agencies was that agents investigating intelligence cases could obtain warrants on lower standards of evidence or probable cause than those working on criminal investigations, so the mixing of information could result in investigators having access to evidence that was improperly obtained. The Patriot Act, however, allowed such sharing of information. It also created links between the CIA (traditionally responsible for foreign intelligence) and the FBI (traditionally responsible for investigating domestic crime), so that the various organizations could cooperate on joint investigations and build a shared database. These measures were intended to remedy the poor interagency communication that was one clear shortcoming in U.S. antiterrorism activities before the 9/11 attacks.

The Patriot Act also amended the nation's immigration laws. It gave the attorney general the power to detain aliens inside the United States—a category that can include legal or illegal immigrants—for seven days without charging them with a crime. Once the Justice Department had filed charges, aliens could be held indefinitely without being told of the charges or given hearings in which to defend themselves. Furthermore, anyone whom the Justice Department suspected had endorsed terrorist activity could be sent out of the country or refused permission to enter it. Endorsement could mean anything from direct membership in a terrorist group such as Al-Qaeda to donating money to a charity that helped fund terrorism, even if the donor did not know of the terrorist connection.

Two Views

In the immediate aftermath of 9/11, it seemed obvious to many Americans that the government should be given whatever it needed to fight terrorism. To quibble about the possible loss of civil liberties while the nation was under attack seemed, to some people, misguided, or even unpatriotic. John Ashcroft, the U.S. attorney general, represented this view when he spoke to the House Committee on the Judiciary on September 24, 2001:

> **Mr. Chairman and members of the committee, the American people do not have the luxury of unlimited time in erecting the necessary defenses to future terrorist acts. The danger that darkened the United States of America and the civilized world on September 11 did not pass with the atrocities committed that day. They require that we provide law enforcement with the tools necessary to identify, dismantle, disrupt, and punish terrorist organizations before they strike again. . . .**
>
> **Now it falls to us, in the name of freedom and those who cherish it, to ensure our nation's capacity to defend ourselves from terrorists. Today I urge the Congress, I call upon the Congress to act, to strengthen our ability to fight this evil wherever it exists . . . .**

Speaking before the same committee on December 6, 2001, Ashcroft responded to those who had pointed out conflicts between the Patriot Act and the Bill of Rights. He said, "[T]o those who scare peace-loving people with phantoms of lost liberty my message is this: Your tactics only aid terrorists, for they erode our national unity and diminish our resolve. They give ammunition to America's enemy and pause to America's friends." In this view, echoed by others in the administration and outside it, criticism of the government and the War on Terror, or efforts

47

to preserve rights such as personal privacy and civil liberties, amounted to strengthening the enemy. Although many people shared this view, the country's population was divided on whether civil liberties should be compromised for the sake of national security.

Between November 2001 and January 2002, a representative sampling of Americans was polled on the question of security versus civil liberties. People were read sets of opposing statements and asked to choose which statement they agreed with. Choices included "'In order to curb terrorism in this country, it will be necessary to give up some civil liberties' or 'We should preserve our freedoms above all, even if there remains some risk of terrorism' and 'Some people say that high school teachers have the right to criticize America's policies toward terrorism' or 'Others say that all high school teachers should defend America's policies in order to promote loyalty to our country.'" Of those polled, 55 percent agreed with the position that freedoms should be preserved above all, while 45 percent said that curbing terrorism was more important. Results for the more specific statements, however, were varied. For example, 40 percent of people took the pro-liberty position that high school teachers are free to criticize the government, but only 8 percent took the pro-security position that the protesters in nonviolent demonstrations against the government should be investigated. A majority of people opposed government monitoring of telephone calls and e-mail, but a majority also supported the introduction of national ID cards. Such results suggested that the American public was divided on the government response to terrorism.

The belief that security from terrorism must be the nation's top priority remained strong in some quarters. In April 2004 an assistant U.S. district attorney named Peter M. Thomson argued that the surveillance provisions of the

Patriot Act were still necessary to protect the country, and that fears about violations of rights were exaggerated. "Moreover," concluded Thomson, "how does the potential loss of privacy to persons over the Internet, for example, compare to the massacre of several thousand persons, the closure of international airspace, the utter destruction of skyscrapers in New York, an economy in a tailspin, and Americans living in terror and afraid to fly on commercial airliners?"

The opposing view had eloquent supporters, too. In an article published in the winter of 2001–2002, legal scholar David Cole wrote:

> **The terrorist attacks of September 11 have shocked and stunned us all and have quite properly spurred renewed consideration of our capability to forestall future attacks. Yet in doing so, we must not rashly trample on the very freedoms that we are fighting for. Nothing tests our commitment to principle like fear and terror. But precisely because the terrorists violated every principle of civilized society and human dignity, we must remain true to our principles as we fashion a response. . . .**
>
> **We must respond to terror, but we must also ensure that our responses are measured and balanced. . . . In other words, freedom and security need not necessarily be traded off against one another; maintaining our freedoms is itself critical to maintaining our security.**

Some of those who disapproved of the broad powers that the Patriot Act had granted to government—specifically, to the executive branch of government—doubted that those powers would, in fact, make Americans safer.

There were also fears that the powers could be misused, as had happened in the past. For example, the Patriot Act gave agencies such as the FBI, CIA, and Treasury greater powers to gather information about people and to review one another's information. Yet advocates for privacy and civil liberties pointed out that federal authorities have not always used intelligence information in just or legal ways. During the 1960s the FBI spied on members of the civil rights movement, including Dr. Martin Luther King Jr. Among other things, FBI agents wiretapped King's phone conversations, threatened him, and leaked information about his personal life in an attempt to smear his reputation. This track record made some people wonder what the government might do with its new, expanded surveillance powers.

Under the Patriot Act, librarians could be required to disclose records of the books patrons had checked out or the Web sites patrons had visited on library computers, and bookstores could be required to turn over records of people's purchases. The idea behind this part of the law was that the act of seeking out certain kinds of information might indicate possible terrorist links, or might be an additional piece of evidence against a suspect. Someone researching bombs and dams, for example, might be planning to blow up a dam. The Patriot Act provided for severe penalties against librarians and bookstore owners who refused to supply the records that were requested, or who told patrons that their records had been checked. Viet Dinh, the assistant attorney general who had helped write the Patriot Act, explained that "libraries and bookstores should not be allowed to become safe havens for terrorists."

Libraries and bookstores became sites of resistance to the Patriot Act. Bookstore owner Neal Coonerty of Santa Cruz, California, said, "We've always argued that what you read is not necessarily who you are. So if you read a murder mystery, it does not mean that you are plotting a murder. Going into bookstores, going into libraries, finding out what people are reading is not really going to make us safer from terrorism." Some librarians and booksellers posted signs warning patrons, "The FBI may be watching what you read." In addition, libraries in some communities took more active measures to protest what they saw as an invasion of privacy. They changed procedures so that patrons' records were shredded or erased from library computers after just a few days.

Profiling

In the hours and days after the 9/11 attacks, President Bush repeatedly urged Americans not to show their anger by attacking the many innocent Middle Eastern, Arab, and Muslim people in the United States. It was the right and honorable thing to do, although, sadly, his words were unable to prevent some brutal assaults. But the question remained: How *would* Americans treat the Muslims, Arabs, and Middle Easterners among them? It was not the first time the United States had been in such a situation.

In the middle of the twentieth century, when the United States was at war with Japan, President Franklin D. Roosevelt took the unprecedented step of ordering that nearly all of the Japanese immigrants and Japanese-American citizens in the western states be rounded up and placed under armed guard in internment camps for the duration of the war. This order was based on the fear—with no evidence—that people of Japanese ancestry living in the United States might aid Japan's war effort by committing acts of espionage or sabotage against the United States. (The western states were targeted because that's where nearly all Japanese Americans lived and because those states were considered most vulnerable to attack from Japan. Although the United States was at war with Germany and Italy in Europe, Americans of German and Italian descent were not forced into camps because, as historians of the war have pointed out, they were white.)

In the 1944 case of *Korematsu v. United States*, the Supreme Court upheld the conviction of a U.S. citizen of Japanese descent who had been arrested and tried because he had not gone to the camp as ordered. The heart of the *Korematsu* case was not Fred Korematsu's loyalty to the United States. That was never questioned. The issue was that he had not allowed himself to be evacuated. The Court maintained that the government had the right to order such an evacuation. In 1988, the U.S. government officially acknowledged that the internment of Japanese Americans had been a tragic mistake. Presidents apologized for it, and the federal government paid reparations—payments in acknowledgment of people's losses or suffering—to the individuals who had been sent to the camps, or to their families. After 9/11, though, some Americans wondered whether Arab Americans should or could be placed under guard.

No mass internment occurred. Many people of Middle Eastern descent, however, were singled out for searches, interrogations, and other forms of official attention that some called ethnic harassment. They were caught up in the phenomenon of profiling, which means singling people out because of their physical characteristics instead of choosing them at random, or based on suspicion of actual wrongdoing.

Racial profiling became a serious problem in U.S. law enforcement in the 1980s and 1990s, when certain police departments and highway patrols singled out greatly disproportionate numbers of African Americans for searches. In some areas, the term *DWB*—"driving while black"—

referred to the fact that a dark-skinned person, especially a young man, was likely to be pulled over for a minor traffic violation, such as a broken taillight, or possibly for no reason at all. The traffic stop would then become an excuse for "fishing"—searching the driver, car, and passengers for drugs or other evidence of crime. After New York City police shot and killed an African-American man named Amadou Diallo in 1999, an outcry against profiling and racially slanted law enforcement caused New York and a number of other cities to pass laws designed to reform police practices. The profiling of people of color did not disappear, however, and after 9/11 it became an issue for people, especially young men, of Middle Eastern appearance.

Airport and airplane security became a tricky problem. The nation had just suffered a devastating blow at the hands of nineteen young Middle Eastern men. No one wanted such a thing to happen again. Anxiety about terrorism—and also, perhaps, anger over what had happened—led to incidents of groundless discrimination against people who appeared Middle Eastern. Men, women, and children were searched repeatedly before being allowed on planes, were refused permission to board, or, in some cases, were removed from planes before takeoff because the other passengers or the pilot objected to their presence.

The Bush administration urgently wanted to restore the nation's air traffic to some semblance of normalcy—a desire shared by the public. Tighter, more consistent security at airports was also clearly needed. In a move meant to achieve both goals, the government declared that all airport security workers would henceforth be federal employees, under the authority of the Transportation Safety Administration (TSA). This included screeners, the people who check passengers and their luggage. The TSA quickly

hired a great many screeners and other security workers—
too quickly, it later appeared. There was little time for
background checks or for adequate training. Some of the
new hires turned out to have criminal records. Many
lacked experience in such matters as frisking and other
physical search techniques, or in ethnic profiling. And because airports were using ethnic profiling to focus on people of Middle Eastern descent, errors were numerous.
Along with giving special attention to Middle Easterners,
screeners targeted Hispanic people, Hindus and Sikhs
from India, Hasidic Jews, and Filipinos, mistaking them
for Middle Easterners because of dark skin, turbans, clothing, or other features.

Mistakes aside, was ethnic profiling justified? Many
people said yes. It was only common sense, given that
the stakes were high, to take special measures against the
group that had produced the hijackers of 9/11 and many
other known terrorists. A little temporary inconvenience,
or even real outrage, on the part of some innocent travelers was outweighed by the possibility of saving hundreds
or thousands of lives by preventing a terrorist from boarding a plane. Supporters of ethnic profiling pointed to El
Al, the national airline of Israel, a nation that has long
been the target of attacks by Arabs and other Muslims. El
Al, which applies stringent ethnic profiling to passengers,
has an excellent security record.

Ethnic profiling received criticism, however, from
Arab-American and Muslim organizations, from rights ad-
vocacy groups such as the American Civil Liberties Union
(ACLU), and from citizens who had been targeted by profiling or who objected to ethnic targeting on principle.
One argument against ethnic profiling was that putting
people in a separate category of suspicion on the basis
of racial or ethnic qualities alone is unfair, unconstitutional, and simply un-American. The United States is still

struggling to overcome other forms of racial and ethnic stereotyping and profiling, such as bias in law enforcement. Why commit the same fault again? Other critics speculated that aggressive ethnic profiling could create resentment, alienation, and even hostility among Muslim or Middle Eastern Americans. Finally, some expressed doubts that additional or more intensive airport questioning and searches—beyond the standard screening through which *all* passengers must pass—would yield any real security benefits.

In time, objections to ethnic profiling, along with lawsuits against it brought by individuals and organizations such as the ACLU, led to the practice being officially ended. It has been replaced in most airports by random searches, in which passengers who are singled out for extra inspection of their persons or their luggage are told that they have been randomly selected by a computer program. In 2003 the Department of Justice issued guidelines on the use of racial and ethnic profiling by federal law enforcement agencies such as the FBI and the TSA. In matters of national security, officials may take race or ethnic background into consideration, but in order to do so, they must have reliable reasons to believe that a specific threat exists and is linked to a particular race or ethnic group.

A case involving Spanish bombings and a fingerprint may bring the issue of profiling under the Patriot Act into a federal courtroom. In March 2004 terrorist bombings of passenger trains in Madrid, Spain, killed 191 people and wounded more than 1,700. Two months later, FBI agents took a Portland, Oregon, attorney named Brandon Mayfield into custody. A fingerprint found on the scene in Madrid had been identified as Mayfield's, they claimed, even though the Spanish authorities did not think the print was a match. Two weeks later, Mayfield was released. A federal court dismissed the case against him, and the FBI

BRANDON MAYFIELD OF PORTLAND, OREGON, IS RELEASED AND CLEARED OF ALL CHARGES AFTER BEING HELD BY U.S. AUTHORITIES WHO MISTAKENLY LINKED HIM TO THE BOMBING OF TRAINS IN MADRID, SPAIN. THE FBI MAY HAVE TARGETED MAYFIELD BECAUSE OF HIS RELIGION: HE IS A CONVERT TO ISLAM.

apologized for a mistaken fingerprint identification. But a report written by the FBI's own inspector general suggests that the FBI held onto Mayfield—and bugged his home and wiretapped his phone conversations—for another reason: he is a convert to Islam. Congressmen John Conyers of Michigan and Robert Scott of Virginia later said, "The report raises real and serious questions regarding racial and ethnic profiling by the FBI as well as their competence, veracity and use of Patriot Act powers."

In late 2004 Mayfield filed suit against the federal government, claiming that his civil liberties had been violated and that parts of the Patriot Act were unconstitutional. Two years later, Mayfield settled part of the claim, receiving a formal apology and $2 million in damages from the government. The settlement also included an agreement that he can continue his legal challenge of the Patriot Act. Mayfield and his attorneys are expected to argue that the FBI's expanded power to carry out secret wiretaps and searches against citizens on the basis of easily obtained FISA warrants is unconstitutional under the Fourth Amendment. The case of mistaken fingerprint identity may put the Patriot Act itself under scrutiny.

Detention Without End

On September 12, 2001, Hady Omar returned to his Arkansas home from a business trip to Florida. The Egyptian-born Omar had just finished greeting his American wife and their American-born daughter when FBI agents and police stormed their house. "They had their hands on their guns," Omar later told CBS News.

Omar was taken into custody, interrogated for seven hours, denied the use of a telephone, and then handcuffed and jailed. Later he was transferred to a maximum-security prison in Louisiana. His wife was not told of his whereabouts, but the next day his town's newspaper featured a prominent article about him, titled "Terror Strikes Home."

Omar spent two months in solitary confinement. The light in his cell was never turned off. The water in the shower was always cold. At one point in his captivity, he was unable to change clothes for two weeks. He was never told why he was being held. "I just start feeling that I'm not going to ever get out of there," said Omar, who at times thought of suicide as the only possible escape from his nightmare.

The only charge ever made against Hady Omar was that he, like thousands of other immigrants—Muslims and others—had overstayed his tourist visa. In other words, he had violated the conditions of his visa, the document that had allowed him to enter the country. He had married a U.S. citizen, obtained a work permit, and applied for the status of permanent U.S. resident, but he had also broken immigration law. In the days before 9/11, such visa violations were generally treated fairly leniently. Although the law allowed the INS to deport visa violators, the agency typically renewed their visas unless there was a reason not to do so, such as a criminal charge. After 9/11, however, federal policy changed. Thousands of Muslims, Arabs, and Middle Easterners were questioned. Visa violations were used as grounds for detaining a thousand or so of them indefinitely, without formal charges.

After two and a half months, Hady Omar was released. Some of those who had been detained were held for much longer periods, or deported to their countries of origin without the chance to appeal their cases or communicate with their families. Nor were all of the detainees foreign nationals. A few, like Nacer Mustafa, were American citizens.

American-born Mustafa was detained on September 15, 2001, when he showed his passport at an airport in Houston, Texas. Officials suspected that the passport had been tampered with, or altered. They also found what seemed to be suspicious elements in Mustafa's background. He had once been found in possession of a large amount of cash, and investigators discovered that he appeared to have two Social Security numbers and two names, possible signs of a secret terrorist identity.

Mustafa spent sixty-seven days in jail while the government investigated his case of passport fraud. His family spent tens of thousands of dollars on legal fees. In the end, the government admitted that it had no case. There was no evidence of passport tampering. One of Mustafa's "aliases" was a nickname. The second Social Security number appeared to be a typo. "What bothered me most," Mustafa told the *New York Times*, "was at the end, they just said I could go. Nobody ever apologized."

In June 2003 the inspector general of the Department of Justice issued a report on the treatment of the hundreds of people who were detained on immigration charges after the antiterrorism dragnets of late 2001 and early 2002. The report acknowledged that there had been widespread and significant violations of detainees' rights and of the law. Some of the detainees were held without charges for months. Some were mistreated, even beaten. Perhaps most troubling, though, was the way the detentions had overturned the principle that people are presumed to be innocent until they are proven to be guilty. The detainees were treated as though their guilt was established by the mere fact that they had been detained. Only after the FBI cleared them—a process that took an average of eighty days—could they be regarded as innocent. This "guilty until proven innocent" approach, the inspector general claimed, was a reversal of the foundation of American justice.

Enemy Combatants and Torture

Questions about detention and detainees' rights resurfaced in connection with enemies captured during military action in Afghanistan and Iraq. On November 13, 2001,

President Bush, in his role as commander in chief of the U.S. military, had issued an order declaring that certain categories of people, if captured, would be tried by military commissions, rather than by criminal courts. The commissions could be secret, if necessary to protect national security interests, and they could issue death penalties. Those who would be tried by commissions were members of Al-Qaeda, people involved in acts of international terrorism against the United States, and people who knowingly harbored such terrorists. The president's military order meant that such people would not enter the nation's public justice system.

The U.S. invasion of Afghanistan resulted in the capture of some Al-Qaeda and Taliban members who, in the opinion of military and intelligence officials, were likely to possess information about the 9/11 attacks or anti-American terrorism in general. These individuals were detained without charges and sent to a U.S. military prison called Camp X-Ray, which is located at Guantánamo Bay, an American base in Cuba. Other suspected terrorists captured by U.S. military forces abroad were also detained at Guantánamo. The treatment of these detainees sparked controversy and accusations of torture.

The core of the controversy was the detainees' status. Were they prisoners of war (POWs)? If so, they were entitled to certain protections and standards of treatment under the Geneva Convention, an international agreement that governs the treatment of captured soldiers. The Bush administration said that the detainees did not meet the Geneva Convention's definition of POWs. They were not members of a recognized military force. They did not wear uniforms or act according to the "rules of war." Calling all detainees "enemy combatants," the administration maintained that they could be held for as long as the government wanted and that U.S. authorities had a fairly free hand in determining how they would be treated.

U.S. MILITARY POLICE AT CAMP X-RAY IN GUANTÁNAMO BAY, CUBA, CARRY A DETAINEE AWAY FROM AN INTERROGATION ROOM. HUMAN-RIGHTS GROUPS HAVE QUESTIONED THE STATUS AND TREATMENT OF THE PEOPLE DETAINED WITHOUT CHARGES AT X-RAY AND OTHER LOCATIONS.

Two human-rights organizations, the International Committee of the Red Cross and Amnesty International (which advocates for prisoners' rights, among other issues), expressed concern about the conditions in which the detainees were kept, charging that their small cells and the restraints they were required to wear while being transferred were unnecessarily inhumane. A fact-finding committee of twenty-five members of Congress that toured Camp X-Ray in January 2002, however, found

Lincoln, Liberty, and the Law in Wartime

War and national security have collided with civil liberty and privacy more than once in U.S. history. President Abraham Lincoln, widely admired as one of the country's great leaders, received sharp criticism for suspending a civil right called *habeas corpus*. Yet he carried out this controversial act during the Civil War, when the nation was locked in combat with itself, because he believed it was necessary to the Union's war effort.

Habeas corpus is part of a Latin phrase that means "you should produce the person to be examined." As a legal principle, it means that someone who is arrested must be brought before a judge and charged with a crime, so that it can be established that the person is being lawfully held. Enshrined as a principle of English law in the seventeenth century, habeas corpus was written into the U.S. Constitution in Article I, Section 9, which reads, in part, "The privilege of the Writ of Habeas Corpus shall not be suspended, unless when cases of Rebellion or invasion the Public Safety may require it." The Constitution clearly allows habeas corpus to be suspended—in other words, it allows people to be arrested and held without charges—in times of rebellion or invasion. The Constitution does not specify, however, *who* may suspend habeas corpus.

When war broke out between North and South in 1861, the border states wavered. In the end, they did not join the South, but many of the people who lived in them wanted the South to win the war. No border state was more important than Maryland, which surrounds Washington, D.C., the capital of the nation—and of the North. In April 1861 President Lincoln ordered one of his generals to arrest any civilians in Maryland who were suspected of urging resistance to the Union. The army rounded up Southern sympathizers, including some who had called for Maryland to join the South and had called on the state's people and soldiers to resist the advance of Union troops. Lincoln's order stated that habeas corpus was suspended in these cases.

The president's order was challenged in court. Roger B. Taney, the chief justice of the Supreme Court, found it unconstitutional. Only Congress, Taney held, was permitted to suspend habeas corpus; the president had acted wrongly in taking such an action on his own. Taney wrote, "The President certainly does not faithfully execute the laws, if he takes upon himself legislative power, by suspending the writ of habeas corpus, and the judicial power also, by arresting and imprisoning a person without due process of law." The president and army ignored the ruling, but less than a year later, Lincoln restored habeas corpus, explaining that he had felt compelled to act decisively. In a crisis, the government had to be free to stamp out treachery before it could do great harm.

Just half a year later, however, Lincoln once again suspended habeas corpus, this time over the entire North. Offenses for which people could be detained now included resisting the military draft. Congress ratified, or voted to accept, this suspension. Critics of Lincoln's action protested in the press, just as many people today have objected to the Bush administration for detaining enemy combatants without legal proceedings. Constitutional scholars and military historians are still arguing over whether Lincoln was right or wrong, and the debate over national security and individual liberties in the War on Terror is likely to last a long, long time. But when a nation perceives itself to be in crisis, rules can become flexible.

"*Inter armas silent leges*," wrote the Roman orator Cicero in the first century BCE. "In war the law is silent."

conditions to be acceptable. Many committee members felt that the international criticism of the camp was exaggerated or based on misinformation.

The question of how the Guantánamo detainees should be treated is complicated by the fact that although some of them may well be innocent of any terrorist acts, others are guilty—or wish to appear so. In early 2007 the Pentagon revealed that a detainee named Waleed Mohammed bin Attash had admitted to planning the attack on the U.S.S. *Cole*, and that Khalid Sheikh Mohammed, who was arrested in a raid in 2003 in Pakistan, had confessed to planning and organizing the 9/11 attacks and to beheading American reporter Daniel Pearl, an atrocity that received worldwide publicity. Although many intelligence experts regard Mohammed's confessions with some mistrust, aware that he might try to glorify his own role in what he regards as a holy war, his confession and those of other Guantánamo detainees suggest that detaining and interrogating foreign suspects has produced results. If the government can hold such individuals indefinitely, however, should the rules be different when the suspects aren't foreign?

Yaser Esam Hamdi was a Guantánamo detainee who had been captured in Afghanistan and accused of being an enemy combatant who was fighting for the Taliban. Hamdi claimed to have been in Afghanistan as a relief worker. At Camp X-Ray, he was found to be a U.S. citizen, and he was then transferred to a military prison in Virginia. Acting on Hamdi's behalf, his father sued Donald Rumsfeld, who was then U.S. secretary of defense, and the Defense Department. Hamdi's claim was that he had been denied the legal rights due to a U.S. citizen. He had not been charged with a specific crime or provided with a lawyer. In 2004 the case of *Hamdi* v. *Rumsfeld* reached the Supreme Court. The Court ruled that U.S.

citizens who have been detained as enemy combatants have the legal right to challenge their detention under the "due process" provision of the Fourteenth Amendment to the Constitution.

A few months earlier, in the similar case of *Padilla v. Rumsfeld*, the Supreme Court had ruled that the president did not have the authority to hold José Padilla, a U.S. citizen, as an enemy combatant without the authorization of Congress. Padilla, who was seized in the United States and not in a combat zone, was suspected of involvement with Al-Qaeda and of planning to make and use a bomb in the United States. After the Court ruled that Padilla could not be held without charges as an enemy combatant, he was transferred to a nonmilitary prison and charged with the criminal offense of supporting terror. Padilla and his attorneys claim that during the time he was detained as an enemy combatant, he suffered abuse and even torture. This mistreatment, Padilla said, made him mentally unfit to stand trial. Federal representatives declared that Padilla's claims of torture are irrelevant to his case, and psychiatric experts presented conflicting evaluations of his mental state. Padilla's trial began in Miami in 2007.

Padilla's is not the only case in which accusations of torture have been raised. At what point does stern treatment become torture? And is torture ever morally justifiable? Americans began asking these questions after news stories started to circulate about terror suspects being seized by the CIA and imprisoned outside the United States. The CIA uses the term *renditions* for these abductions of non-U.S. citizens who are suspected of having information about terrorist activities. The subjects of rendition are detained in countries that are known to lack strict human rights protections. Michael Scheuer, a former CIA agent who claimed to have participated in numerous renditions, told the CBS news program *60 Minutes* that officials understood that renditions to places such as Egypt would result in torture of the suspects. According to Scheuer, renditions began in the 1990s, during the administration of President Bill Clinton.

Evidence that the federal government was prepared to defend itself against accusations of torture emerged in the form of a memo that had been prepared in 2002 for Alberto Gonzales, attorney general of the United States. Written by an assistant attorney general, the memo outlined ways that *torture* could be defined under U.S. and international law. It also presented possible defenses that could be used against claims that federal or military interrogation methods had crossed the line into torture. The memo's author concluded that "certain acts may be cruel, inhuman, and degrading, but still not produce pain and suffering of the requisite intensity" to qualify as torture.

Torture is the ultimate violation of privacy—a deliberate assault on body or mind that is intended to cause severe pain or to "break" someone's mind or personality. Many people regard the use of torture, no matter what the provocation or purpose, as a barbaric and unacceptable act, one that reduces the torturer to a moral level below that of his captive. There is also a practical objection. The majority of experts in interrogation consider information gained under torture to be worthless, or at least of doubtful value, because people will say anything to stop the torture. Another objection is that if the United States condones torture of its foreign prisoners, it has no valid ground for objecting to the torture of Americans by foreigners.

The "ticking time bomb" argument is often put forward in defense of torture—or at least of making torture a possible option. If you had good reason to believe that a terrorist had hidden a bomb that would soon explode, killing hundreds or perhaps thousands of people, how far would you go to learn the location of the bomb? If you had good reason to think that a prisoner might possess that information, what would you do to get it? Would the psychological or physical torture of one person be too high a price to pay for saving many lives? Or does torture cross a moral line that should never be crossed? Finally, there is the question of whether torture would work. Perhaps the terrorist would give false information in order to bring the pain to an end, or would simply endure pain rather than confessing. Suicide bombers believe that dying for their cause will bring a heavenly reward. Someone who shares such a belief may be willing and able to withstand torture.

Some Americans are repelled by the notion that their government would condone any form of abusive treatment, even if it fell short of technical definitions of torture. Others, however, feel that terrorists have placed themselves outside the standards of civilized behavior, and that the need to protect innocent lives must outweigh other considerations. But what if mistakes are made?

Maher Arar, a Syrian-born Canadian citizen, was returning from a family vacation in the North African nation of Tunisia when he changed planes at a New York airport in 2002. There he was seized by CIA agents and flown first to Jordan, then to Syria. Suspected of being a terrorist, Arar was tortured for ten months, he claims, and then released. The Canadian government was skeptical of his story, but after an investigation that lasted more than two years, it determined that he was innocent of terrorism ties. Inexperienced and overenthusiastic Canadian law enforcement officials had mistakenly passed his name to U.S. intelligence. Steven Harper, Canada's prime minister, apologized to Arar, and the Canadian government paid him a large reparation. Arar is not alone. In 2003 a German citizen was kidnapped by CIA agents and physically abused in

Afghanistan for months in a rendition that the CIA later called a case of mistaken identity. As other bungled renditions come to light, Americans may be forced to reconsider the value of this antiterror strategy.

The Patriot Act—Again

When the Patriot Act was passed into law in 2001, it contained a sunset provision. Parts of the act would expire—in effect, the sun would set on them—after five years, unless Congress reauthorized them. As the time of reauthorization drew near, supporters and critics of the act communicated their views to the House of Representatives and the Senate. Responding to concern that the Patriot Act infringed on civil liberties, Congress revised some parts of it and added new elements. These changes were aimed at safeguarding people's rights.

With the reforms in place, Congress reauthorized the act, and President Bush signed it into law on March 9, 2006. Under a new sunset provision, three clauses of the act will expire in 2009 unless reauthorized. One clause lets investigators request court orders that will give them access to private information, such as library records, without having to show that the person being investigated is suspicious. Another clause permits "John Doe roving wiretaps," in which agents can listen in on phone conversations without having reason to believe that the person using the phone is a suspected terrorist. The third lets federal officials monitor foreign citizens in the United States without showing that they are acting on behalf of a foreign power.

The reauthorized Patriot Act also gave federal agents stronger powers to demand people's financial, telephone, and Internet use records without a court order—although businesses that are ordered to turn over customers' or employees' records have the right to consult with lawyers. Under the reauthorized act, agents are still permitted to request secret search warrants for any home or business, without evidence of a connection to terrorism. After reauthorization, the ACLU declared, "The amended Patriot Act fails to adequately protect the privacy rights of innocent, ordinary people in this country." Yet the bill to renew the act had passed in both houses of Congress, and many people shared the view of President Bush, who said after signing it, "The terrorists have not lost the will or the ability to attack us. The Patriot Act is vital to the war on terror and defending our citizens against a ruthless enemy."

4

Under Surveillance

If you were living in a cage, you would know it, wouldn't you? Maybe not, says social critic and historian Christian Parenti. He believes that Americans are being encaged, one bar at a time, but the cage is not made of steel. Parenti calls it the "soft cage"—the invisible web of surveillance.

Surveillance is not new. In his 2003 book *The Soft Cage: Surveillance from Slavery to the War on Terror*, Parenti shows that those in power have always had ways of tracking people's movements and monitoring their activities. And surveillance is not always a bad thing. From hall passes in schools to the security video camera whose footage—broadcast on the television show *America's Most Wanted* in 2002—led to the identification and capture of a bank robber, many surveillance tools serve useful, even necessary, functions. Today, however, technology can capture more information about what we do and where we go than George Orwell could have imagined when he was writing *1984*. One possibility is that, in a climate of anxiety about crime, terrorism, and safety, people will agree to a degree of surveillance they may later regret but find hard to reverse. Another possibility is that they may come under that degree of surveillance themselves without even knowing it.

Privacy Laws and Privacy Flaws

During the turbulent 1960s and early 1970s, America's social and political landscape was reshaped by forces such as the civil rights movement for racial equality and the movement to end the Vietnam War. There were protest marches, demonstrations, sit-ins, and student takeovers of university campuses. Major cities erupted in race riots. Large numbers of people were questioning authority. At the same time, the public was becoming increasingly aware that the government possessed a great deal of information about its citizens. Some of that information was gathered in the course of normal federal business, such as administering the armed forces, the Department of Education, and pension and welfare programs. Other information was collected by covert means. FBI agents, for example, infiltrated protest marches, saw who was present, and then spied on the protesters.

Responding to growing concern about the scope and use of government records, Congress passed the Freedom of Information Act (FOIA) in 1966. This law requires the government to release information and documents about government activities upon request. Exceptions include personnel files, medical files, financial information, and most information connected with national security or law enforcement; in fulfilling an FOIA request, a federal agency may withhold or obliterate pieces of information that fall into these categories.

People have used FOIA requests for all kinds of purposes. Vietnam veterans have found information about chemicals to which they were exposed during the war.

THE FREEDOM OF INFORMATION ACT (FOIA) GIVES THE PUBLIC ACCESS TO GOVERNMENT DOCUMENTS—BUT WITH LIMITS. FOR A REPORT ON HIV AND AIDS IN PRISON, A PRESS ORGANIZATION REQUESTED AUTOPSY REPORTS ON INMATES, BUT THE RELEVANT INFORMATION WAS BLACKED OUT.

UFO conspiracy theorists have gained access to U.S. Air Force investigations of alleged sightings of alien spacecraft. Biographers have uncovered FBI files on public figures such as John Lennon of the Beatles.

Alarm about the FBI spying on citizens flared up again after the Watergate scandal of the 1970s. The Watergate case exploded into the headlines after President Richard Nixon was shown to have used federal employees for covert intelligence actions, including illegal wiretapping and break-ins, against people he considered his enemies. Partly in response to this revelation, Congress passed the Privacy Act of 1974. The Privacy Act extended the FOIA concept to files on individual citizens. It requires the government to notify people when it collects or stores information about them, and it lets people review the files the government maintains on them, with exceptions. The act also allows people to correct their records if they are inaccurate, and it entitles them to sue the government if their information has been misused—say, released to someone else. In 1996 Congress added an amendment to FOIA that requires federal agencies to maintain FOIA Web pages and to make some documents available online by request.

Other laws have been crafted to plug particular privacy leaks. The Driver's Privacy Protection Act of 1994, for example, prohibits Department of Motor Vehicle (DMV) employees from releasing personal information about people who have driver's licenses. The stimulus for this law was the 1989 murder of a young actress named Rebecca Schaefer. She was killed by a stalker who had hired a private detective to get her address; the detective had obtained it from the California DMV. The law created to protect DMV information, however, contains many exceptions—including one that gives private detectives access to drivers' information.

Medical information is another highly sensitive form of data that is vulnerable to misuse. Some medical information could cause hardship or embarrassment to people if wrongly released. An employer might be reluctant to hire someone who had been treated for heart trouble, diabetes, or depression, for example. Someone who had visited a doctor in connection with a sexually transmitted disease might be horrified to receive mail at home from a pharmaceutical company that is marketing a drug for treating that disease. Medical information does not have to concern potentially sensitive subjects such as sexually transmitted diseases or mental illness to deserve protection, however. Most people feel that their family's medical records, even those dealing with ordinary problems such as the flu, are no business of outsiders.

Federal protection for health information falls under the Health Insurance Portability and Accountability Act of 1996 (HIPAA). The act protects the rights of workers to maintain health insurance when they change jobs or lose their jobs, but it also contains provisions that govern the ways institutions such as hospitals, billing services, and insurance companies handle medical records.

A provision called the Privacy Act was added to HIPAA in 2003. Before the Privacy Act, health-care providers were supposed to get patients' consent before disclosing the patients' medical or health information to third parties. The Privacy Act removed the requirement of patients' consent in some cases, allowing providers to disclose information for what the act calls "treatment, payment, or health care operations." Under the act, a patient's medical information may be freely shared with other health-care providers; with corporations that own and operate hospitals and other health-care businesses; with billing services, bill-collection agencies, or other businesses connected with health-care administration; and with some government agencies. Providers of health care are required to notify patients that such disclosures may occur.

Patients, on the other hand, can prohibit some uses of their medical information. They have the right to forbid disclosure of their information to marketers or to employers. The Privacy Act also requires all health-care providers and other entities that maintain or handle medical information to create plans for safeguarding the information, whether it exists in a manila folder or an electronic file.

Public health and national security needs—such as a fast-spreading disease epidemic or a case of biological or chemical terrorism—can override patient privacy. In such cases, health-care providers work with the federal Centers for Disease Control and Prevention (CDC), and possibly with law enforcement agencies. Authorities try to identify relevant cases, create a timeline, and pinpoint the source of the problem, as well as locate people who might require treatment.

One particular type of medical information offers unique advantages in law enforcement but raises questions about privacy. Genetic information can be an invaluable tool in identifying a criminal (or in proving a suspect's innocence). Like a fingerprint, the DNA in skin cells, saliva, blood, and other tissues is a unique identifier for each individual. For years, law enforcement agencies have been collecting samples of blood and other materials that can be used for DNA testing. Standards for collection vary from state to state. Sex offenders must supply DNA samples in all states, but felons and juveniles must do so in only some states.

The DNA profiles of convicted criminals are entered in an FBI database known as the Combined DNA Index System (CODIS), a national pool of information that is available to local, state, and federal law enforcement agencies. But what about samples collected from suspects or persons who were present at a crime scene but who were never convicted, or even arrested? There is no universal standard for how these samples, and the genetic profiles drawn from them, are to be treated. Federal and state law enforcement groups, in general, want to add this DNA information to a central database. Some have even called for the creation of a DNA database on all Americans. Such an information pool would revolutionize criminal investigation, making it possible to identify the source of any biological evidence, from a stray hair to a drop of blood. A DNA database would also make it far more difficult for people to operate under false identities. If someone's identity was in doubt, a DNA test would resolve the matter. In the same way, the database would greatly simplify the identification of lost children and recovered kidnap victims.

Privacy advocates, however, argue that the government has no business maintaining genetic records of citizens who have not committed crimes. One reason not to expand DNA databases unnecessarily, according to the Electronic Privacy Information Center (EPIC), is that such information is vulnerable to abuse. The data could be leaked or stolen, or new laws could allow it to be used in unforeseen ways, with far-reaching effects on people's lives. DNA is much more than a genetic fingerprint. It can provide information about ethnic background, family relationships, and vulnerability to certain diseases or conditions. Some researchers think that even kinds of behavior, such as addiction and violence, may be linked to genetics. According to this view, DNA doesn't guarantee that an individual will become an addict or a killer, but it may suggest a higher than average risk of that fate.

Even when such connections are unproven, they could be used against individuals. An insurance company might deny coverage to people whose DNA reveals them to be at elevated risk for cancer, for example, or a company might decide not to hire someone whose genetic profile suggests a possibility of future addiction. Could genetic screening even be used someday to prevent people from having children if their DNA showed a likelihood of birth defects or disease in their offspring? In early 2007 several committees in the U.S. House of Representatives and Senate held hearings on a proposed Genetic Information Nondiscrimination Act (GINA). If passed, the act would ban discrimination based on genetic information in employment, housing, credit, and other areas covered by federal antidiscrimination laws.

Technological advances and changing circumstances can raise new concerns about both privacy and security. The limits of both are generally tested in courts of law. In June 2001, for example, the U.S. Supreme Court heard the case of *Kyllo* v. *United States*. A federal agent had suspected that a Florence, Oregon, man named Dale Kyllo was growing marijuana in his home, an activity that typically requires the use of high-intensity lights that radiate a significant amount of heat, or infrared radiation. Using a thermal imaging device, which detects infrared radiation and produces an image of "hot spots," the agent scanned the suspect's home from the street. The scan showed unusual heat patterns. Based in part on the thermal scan, the agent got a search warrant, entered the suspect's home, and found marijuana plants growing under special lights. Kyllo appealed the agent's use of thermal imaging all the way to the Supreme Court.

The case before the Court was not whether Kyllo was guilty of growing marijuana. It was whether the agent's use of the thermal imaging device—before he had a warrant—was constitutional. Did it violate the Constitution's Fourth Amendment protection against unreasonable searches and seizures?

"It would be foolish to contend that the degree of privacy secured to citizens by the Fourth Amendment has been entirely unaffected by the advance of technology," wrote Justice Antonin Scalia in the Court's opinion. "The question we confront today is what limits there are on this power of technology to shrink the realm of guaranteed privacy." The Court found that the thermal scan had been unconstitutional. In using "a device that is not in general public use, to explore details of the home that would previously have been unknowable without physical intrusion," the agent had conducted a search and therefore should have obtained a warrant first.

The Court's ruling drew what Justice Scalia called a "bright line" around private homes, which deserve the fullest Fourth Amendment protection. But if the case had been heard a few months later, after the terrorist attacks on New York City and Washington, D.C., and if federal attorneys had argued that thermal imaging could be used to fight terrorism in some way, might *Kyllo* v. *United States* have been decided differently?

Domestic Surveillance

When the U.S. government announced the "War on Terror" after 9/11, it was clear that the war would be fought within U.S. borders as well as beyond them. The Patriot Act was a major weapon in the war, but the government also introduced programs designed to bring the American public under various kinds of surveillance.

One program promoted by the Department of Justice was called the Terrorist Information and Prevention System (TIPS). Its purpose was to encourage Americans to be attentive to signs of suspicious activity—or, as critics put it, to spy on each other. TIPS was intended to start with a million or so service workers, such as postal carriers, utility meter readers, and truck drivers. In the course of their daily activities, such people would be in a good position to notice mysterious packages, sudden or unusual gatherings of people, or other things that might be signs of a terrorist plot. In time, neighborhood groups would be added to the program.

Civil liberties groups and some congressional lawmakers opposed TIPS. They claimed that at best it would lead to a huge amount of meaningless snooping and snitching. At worst, it would make people unduly suspicious of each other and encourage a vigilante attitude that might lead to harassment of Middle Easterners or Muslims. TIPS was scrapped before it was implemented.

As part of the heightened security measures for air travel after 9/11, the Department of Homeland Security and Transportation Safety Administration beefed up an earlier baggage-screening program called the Computer Assisted Passenger Prescreening System (CAPPS). The revised version, known as CAPPS II, was intended to take effect when a passenger checked in to receive his or her boarding pass, before getting on an airplane. Each passenger would be asked to provide some information that had not previously been part of airline check-ins, such as home telephone number and address. CAPPS would then comb publicly or commercially available databases as well as government security files for information about the passenger. Based on the results of this operation, which was expected to take only a few seconds, the program would give each passenger one of three risk scores: no threat, unknown or possible threat, or high risk. Passengers who were known or suspected terrorists, whose information suggested a false identity, or who were revealed to have outstanding warrants for violent crimes, would be approached by federal agents before they could board the plane.

CAPPS and its revised version, CAPPS II, never got off the ground, despite the fact that the government spent more than $100 million developing the program. Critics in civil liberties organizations, as well as some members of Congress, found the program both excessively intrusive and potentially ineffective. In 2004 CAPPS II was suspended. The Transportation Security Administration announced plans for a new passenger-screening program to be called Secure Flight. Congress insisted that such a program must meet certain privacy and accuracy standards. Secure Flight was initially expected to be ready for testing by 2005, but in 2007 the TSA announced that the $140 million program would be delayed until at least 2010 after government reports indicated problems with both privacy and effectiveness.

Unlike programs that are designed to obtain information from all travelers, watch lists and no-fly lists originate with intelligence agencies. These rosters give officials the names of people who have been identified as terrorists, or who are suspected of aiding terrorists or having ties to terrorist organizations. Anyone who enters or leaves the country, attempts to board a plane, or is stopped for a traffic violation may have his or her name checked against these lists. Someone whose name appears on a roster may receive extra screening and searching at airports, or may not be allowed to fly at all, ever, on a U.S. plane.

Watch lists and no-fly lists serve an undeniable security purpose, but problems can occur when someone's name gets placed on the list by mistake, or when someone has the same name as someone on the list. This has happened on many occasions. Even members of Congress have experienced the problem: Senator Ted Kennedy of Massachusetts and Representatives John Lewis of Georgia and Don Young of Alaska have run into problems at airports because their travel documents triggered an alarm with a watch list. Between 2003 and 2006 the number of names on terrorism watch lists grew from 75,000 to 325,000. A government report indicated that by 2006 more than

30,000 people had suffered false positive identifications—in other words, they were mistakenly identified with names on the watch lists.

Warrantless wiretapping may be the most controversial of the government's domestic surveillance programs. In 2005 information came to light about a secret program authorized by President Bush soon after 9/11. The president authorized a federal intelligence organization called the National Security Agency (NSA) to monitor people's telephone calls and emails without warrants—not even the secret Foreign Intelligence Surveillance Act (FISA) warrants that are supposed to be used under the Patriot Act. The NSA surveillance actions were carried out on the basis of executive orders from the president alone. In 2006 the ACLU filed a lawsuit against the NSA, charging that warrantless surveillance is unconstitutional. The case is expected to reach the Supreme Court. Meanwhile, in early 2007 the government announced that the NSA would begin getting FISA warrants for wiretaps.

Intelligence gathering, surveillance, and espionage are vital if terrorism is to be effectively combated. Yet some worry that in its quest to identify terror threats, the government is casting too wide a net—or possibly using the terror threat as an excuse for broader surveillance in general. FOIA requests by the ACLU and others have shown that the Pentagon has compiled surveillance files on peace activists and others who have protested the war in Iraq. The FBI has investigated people because they belong to groups such as the environmental organization Greenpeace and People for the Ethical Treatment of Animals (PETA). Do such investigations serve any real national security purpose? What is to prevent those in power from using the nation's intelligence agencies to investigate their political opponents, as happened when the FBI secretly monitored Martin Luther King Jr.? Should those who are entrusted with the vital task of protecting people from terrorism be governed by checks and balances? The ancient Roman poet Juvenal put the question in a way that remains timely today: "*Quis custodiet custodes ipsos?*" Who watches the watchers?

Data Mining

Miners look for bits of precious metal in masses of rocky ore. Data miners look for nuggets of useful information in the vast universe of digital data. Data mining is a form of surveillance that focuses on the electronic world of databases and cyberspace.

The amount of readily available information on most people is surprising, and may be frightening. Some of it is available through very low-tech methods. According to security and technology consultant David H. Holtzman, author of *Privacy Lost: How Technology Is Endangering Your Privacy* (2006), "dumpster diving," or going through trash, is one of the most effective ways for police, private detectives, intelligence agents, identity thieves, or paparazzi to gather some kinds of information. "A family's life can easily be pieced together by sorting through discarded packaging, medicine bottles, and food containers," he says. Once trash leaves private property, it is not protected by privacy laws.

There are less messy ways to get much of the same information, or more. Many companies keep records of their customers' purchases. Supermarket chains, for example, issue cards to the customers that entitle them to sale prices and other benefits; the cards also create a database of each customer's purchases. Airline frequent-flyer programs keep records of people's travels. If you've ever bought books, music, or other products from online vendors such as Amazon.com, you have probably been invited to create a customer profile that lets you track the status of your orders. It also lets the vendor greet you by name the next time you visit and suggest things you might be interested in buying, based on records of what you've bought—or even looked at—on past visits.

Public records such as birth and death announcements, home sales or purchases, graduation lists, and information about court cases also contain personal information that is of great value to marketers. When ads for baby food and coupons for diapers start arriving in the mail of parents who have just brought a new baby home from the hospital, a marketer has been at work. Marketers and advertisers often buy customer lists from companies called data aggregators, who acquire, store, and sort massive amounts of data and then sift it to produce customized reports. Large aggregators such as ChoicePoint and Acxiom maintain billions upon billions of pieces of data about people. Another information provider, Experian, has claimed to possess more than a thousand pieces of information on each of 98 percent of American households.

Whenever data is stored, there exists the danger that it can be lost, stolen, or misused. ChoicePoint, for example, has on more than one occasion been scammed into selling data to criminals posing as businesses. Because records held by aggregators may include addresses, Social Security numbers, and credit reports, they can be used as the basis for identity theft. One of the thieves of the ChoicePoint data sold identities for $45 to $60 each. Another firm, Metromail, used prisoners to enter information into its database, giving convicted criminals access to data on thousands of Americans. In one case, a woman received a threatening letter from one of the prison workers, a rapist and thief who knew many details of her personal life, from her address to her favorite magazines.

Privacy and consumer advocates regard the safe

management of these huge commercial databases as a growing crisis. Although some states now require companies that collect information on people to notify individuals when their data has been leaked or stolen, the data industry is unevenly regulated. The problem of data protection, some observers think, is likely to worsen.

Data mining isn't just for marketers. It plays a role in national security and law enforcement, although that role is sometimes shadowy and controversial. The Drug Enforcement Agency (DEA) has searched through supermarkets' shopping data looking for customers who buy unusually large numbers of small plastic bags, which are often used to hold drugs. Federal agents used shopping records and other information about Mohammed Atta, one of the 9/11 terrorists, to create a profile of a terrorist's tastes. There is no reason to believe that the agents have used the profile to identify shoppers with similar tastes and investigate them, but the existence of the profile raises the question of whether someone should be investigated on the basis of food choices.

Data mining was part of an ambitious security program developed by the Defense Department after 9/11. Called Total Information Awareness (TIA), the program would require every private, commercial, and government database in the United States to make its information available to federal intelligence agencies. Records of people's communication, shopping, utility bills, travel, education, and health care would be merged into a central database that could be sorted and searched for suspicious patterns—frequent trips to the Middle East, perhaps, combined with the purchase of a boxcutter and a reading list that included books critical of the U.S. government. When the name Total Information Awareness created a negative impression, making too many people think of Orwell's all-knowing, all-powerful Big Brother, the Defense Department renamed the program Terrorist Information Awareness. It was a shrewd public relations move, but it wasn't enough. In 2003 Congress shut down funding for TIA until the Defense Department could produce detailed reports on how it would handle the privacy issues related to the program. Federal agencies may, however, buy commercially available data from the same aggregators that sell it to marketers.

The Internet is another arena where security and privacy clash, in part because the legal standards of privacy protection for Internet communications and activities are still being hammered out in court cases and legal challenges. Voice Over Internet Protocol (VOIP) technology is one example. VOIP programs allow people to make voice calls, like telephone calls, over the Internet rather than by dialing phone numbers. Is a conversation made using VOIP a phone call, or is it an Internet communication? Currently, telephone calls have a higher standard of protection from police or federal eavesdropping than Internet communications, so privacy advocates want VOIP to be regulated like telephone calls. Law enforcement and intelligence groups, however, argue that VOIP falls under the rules that govern Internet eavesdropping.

Long before 9/11, federal agencies were datatapping Internet communications to and from people suspected of crime or terrorism. One FBI program, known as Carnivore, started to receive press coverage in 2000. To use Carnivore, the FBI installed software at Internet Service Providers (ISPs) to intercept and monitor the incoming and outgoing e-mails of suspects, as well as track their activities on the Web. Carnivore was designed to sniff out only the communications and activities associated with specific users, and agents needed a court order or warrant to use it. Many ISPs challenged the FBI in court over the program, and lost.

After 9/11, the Patriot Act broadened the FBI's ability to install and use Carnivore. At the same time, however, some published reports said that the program was becoming less useful because it did not work on e-mails and other files that had been encrypted by users who used special software to encode their data. According to some accounts, Carnivore has been replaced by other programs, although Internet monitoring remains a key part of national security. Federal agencies are rumored to possess a program called Magic Lantern, which does not operate at the ISP. Instead it infiltrates a suspect's computer, like a virus or Trojan horse, and then operates from within, recording the activities on the computer. Little information is publicly available on this or any related program.

Debates continue over where to draw the line between security and privacy in cyberspace. In February 2007, for example, a bill was introduced into the House of Representatives that was aimed at limiting access to child pornography. It included a provision that would prevent ISPs from deleting or purging their records of subscribers' Web activities. Law enforcement can order a specific ISP to retain its data, but some agencies have pressed for a universal law requiring data to be retained. The Center for Democracy and Technology (CDT), an organization that advocates for civil liberties in cyberspace, had argued that requiring all ISPs to retain data would lead to massive accumulations of information that would be vulnerable to hacking and identity theft. The CDT also warned of "mission creep," meaning that data that is preserved today for use in investigations of child pornography may be used tomorrow for other purposes that were not named when the law came into existence.

ISPs provide access to the Internet, but they are not the only sources of information about what people do online. Companies that operate search engines such as Google and

Yahoo maintain massive databases that show which search terms people have entered, what links they have followed, and which Web pages they have accessed by means of the search engines. The data could be used in various ways. Search-term usage could be surveyed to determine, for example, how many times a particular search term, such as *anthrax*, was accessed by all users during a particular time period. But search-engine databases could also link particular searches to their source computers, although there is no evidence that this is being done. Whether search data should be destroyed, protected, or made available to the government is becoming a hotly debated issue on the electronic frontier. If the possibility exists that authorities can identify a terrorist by the pattern of his search terms, should everyone be willing to have the records of their searches scanned?

E-mail privacy is never guaranteed. Once the "send" button has been hit, the sender has no absolute guarantee that the e-mail will not be intercepted, or that the person who receives it will not forward it or lose control of it in some way. E-mails are also deliberately monitored, far more often than most people realize—by their bosses. According to the American Management Association, more than three-quarters of U.S. companies keep tabs on their employees' on-the-job Internet use, including the personal e-mails they send or receive. Employer tracking of Internet use during company time, on company computers, is not a violation of privacy under the law, although it remains to be seen how employers will deal with workers who use their personal handheld wireless computing devices when on the job.

Employees have created their own disasters by sending indiscreet or crude e-mails to friends who forwarded them to other friends . . . and before the original sender knew it, his or her e-mail was read by millions of people on popular

Web sites. People have been fired from their jobs after e-mails that were critical of their employers or insulting to their coworkers were posted online. In the age of the Internet, the distinction between "work" and "private life" can become blurred.

Who's Watching?

Ten neighbors in Sacramento, California, pooled their money to install a $2,400 video surveillance camera on the courtyard where they lived. Footage from the camera later played a role in the capture of a suspected rapist and murderer. Such incidents are a powerful argument for the benefits of video surveillance.

Most surveillance cameras are installed not just in the expectation that they will provide crime-solving clues, but in the hope that their presence will deter, or prevent, people from committing crimes in the first place. Video monitoring, or closed-circuit television (CCTV), has been used for years as a security measure in places such as banks, museums, and parking garages. CCTV was on the rise well before 9/11, but the terror attacks spurred an increase in the number of cameras used for surveillance in public areas: streets, playgrounds, parks, schools, sports stadiums, and, of course, airports. Additional cameras have also sprouted around bridges, reservoirs, power plants, dams, and other structures that could be vulnerable to attack.

Video recording of public activities is legal in the United States and many other countries, as long as the camera does not intrude into people's private property, and as long as people are not recorded in settings where they have reasonable expectations of privacy, such as restrooms or dressing rooms. Most Americans can expect to be captured by multiple surveillance cameras during a

CLOSED CIRCUIT TELEVISIONS IN LONDON'S SUBWAY STATIONS AND BUSES CAPTURED THESE IMAGES OF SUSPECTS IN A FAILED 2005 BOMBING ATTEMPT. THE IMAGES HELPED AUTHORITIES IDENTIFY AND ARREST THE MEN.

typical day outside their homes, especially if they are city dwellers. During a single visit to an average-sized mall, for example, you are likely to be recorded a dozen times or more.

Since the 1990s the people of Great Britain have been testing the costs and benefits of living in a surveillance society. Britain embraced CCTV after two terrorist bombings and a horrific crime shook the nation. In 1993 and 1994, bombs planted by the Irish Republican Army (IRA) went off in a part of London called the City, a historic and crowded area that is the country's financial center. To prevent more such attacks, or at least to give authorities a better chance of identifying the bombers if more attacks took place, the government announced that the City would be protected by a "ring of steel," a network of CCTV cameras to record everyone who entered or left the district.

Also in 1993, two ten-year-old boys kidnapped a two-year-old child from a shopping center and murdered him. A security camera captured images of the two boys leading the child away, and this sight added to the nation's horror. Although the image was too poor in quality for the boys to be identified and played no role in solving the crime, many people felt that more cameras, or better ones, might somehow have helped to prevent the tragedy. Over the years that followed, the government spent more than three-quarters of the money budgeted for crime prevention to promote the installation of CCTV systems in communities across the land. Seventy-nine British cities had CCTV surveillance systems in their central districts in 1994. Four years later, the number had jumped to 440.

The number of cameras kept growing as police and civic government divisions, commercial real-estate operators such as the owners of shopping centers and office buildings, transportation systems, and neighborhood councils installed cameras and monitoring systems. Because there are hundreds or thousands of systems that operate independently, the total number of surveillance cameras in Britain's public spaces cannot be known for certain, but by 2006 researchers estimated that there were at least five million of them, or one for every twelve people in the land. The average inhabitant of Great Britain, they estimated, was photographed about three hundred times each day. Britain may be the most heavily surveilled nation on Earth, but others are following close behind. CCTV is on the rise in a number of European and Asian countries as well as in the United States.

Video surveillance was expected to serve several related but different purposes. First, cameras would record events. If a crime took place, law enforcement officials could use images from the cameras to identify the criminal. Many identifications have been made in this way, but the process can be time-consuming. Scanning thousands of frames of images from multiple cameras, and obtaining a usable image from them, does not happen as quickly in real life as it does on television crime shows, even with the aid of computers. It can take days. But if an operator watches the input from the cameras as events unfold, he or she can alert police that someone is breaking into a parked car or leaving a suspicious-looking package in a railway station's trash container. In this way, criminals and terrorists can be nabbed on the spot. The real hope, though, is that CCTV is a deterrent to crime and terrorism. Knowing that they are being watched and recorded, people will hesitate to break the law. Thousands of signs in public places across Britain drive home the message: "CCTV: Watching for You!"

CCTV's scope in Britain soon extended far beyond terrorism and violent crime. Cameras now record the license plates of cars in areas where drivers are required to pay special traffic taxes. Combined with motion detectors, cameras record the plates of cars that speed or run stop lights, a law enforcement practice that is increasingly common in the United States. Some CCTV systems are equipped with "smart software" programmed to recognize faces or search subjects' behavior for anything that seems odd or unusual. Gait recognition programs, now under de-

Spying in the Home

Parents who leave a young child in the hands of a nanny while they're at work may wonder how the nanny treats their child when they're not around. Thanks to affordable home spy equipment, they can find out. A generation or so ago, a tiny, concealed surveillance camera that could record everything that happened in a room for hours on end would have seemed like something out of an espionage novel or a movie. Today stores and Web sites sell such devices to ordinary people at discount prices.

Nannycams, as they are sometimes called, let parents keep an eye on how caregivers treat their children. Parents install one or more cameras in key locations in their homes, such as the living room, kitchen, and baby's room; if the parents intend to keep the cameras secret, the cameras may be hidden or disguised as clocks, smoke alarms, books, or other objects. Some cameras simply record what happens, producing films that the parents can play back later on a television or computer. Increasingly common, though, are live-feed cameras that send a signal to a remote computer. The parent can access that computer from any Internet connection to see what's happening at home at that moment.

No one knows how many nannycams lurk on shelves and mantelpieces across America, with or without the knowledge of the child-care workers who are their targets. Millions have been sold. In 2003 a woman who does background checks and video surveillance on nannies reported that the surveillance part of her business was increasing by 20 to 30 percent a year. To parents who employ the technology, it brings peace of mind. It can, however, bring danger. Wireless broadcasts from some nanny-cams may be able to be intercepted by strangers, exposing the interior of the home to prying or criminal eyes. Privacy rights are also an issue. Should in-home workers be told that they are being filmed? What if a nanny chooses to clean house in her underwear when the children are not around? Does capturing her on film violate her privacy?

Not according to the law. It is legal everywhere in the United States for people to secretly take pictures or films in their own homes, without telling the people who may be caught on camera. Fifteen states, however, have laws against making sound recordings of people without their knowledge, even on private property.

Spycams are bought by plenty of people who don't employ nannies. Some high-end home security systems include live camera monitoring as part of their protection against break-ins. Domestic espionage plays a part, too. People have installed cameras to keep tabs on their spouses or to monitor their children's activities.

One mother in Gresham, Oregon, installed cameras in the rooms of her twelve-year-old daughter and fourteen-year-old son. "The cameras aren't hidden," she explains. "I told them up front that I was doing it. It's partly for their protection, in case someone breaks in, and yes, it's partly so that I can know that neither of them is doing something they shouldn't. I can't control what they do when they're away from home, but there are so many pitfalls in being a teenager today, I have to do what I can when they're home."

What do the kids think of the cameras? Says the boy, "It's a sign that she doesn't trust me, and now I feel like I don't trust her, either." Adds his sister, "Kids deserve some privacy. I shouldn't be spied on in my own room." As surveillance gear becomes smaller and cheaper, debates about if, when, and how it's okay to spy at home are likely to continue.

velopment, are supposed to analyze the motions of people caught on camera and determine whether any of the subjects are walking in a strange or suspicious manner. In 2006 the city of Middlesbrough became the first in Britain to use "speaking CCTV"—cameras equipped with loudspeakers that issue warnings to people who are doing what the *New Statesman*, a British magazine, called "acting antisocially," such as littering or committing vandalism. When Brendan O'Neill, author of an article on CCTV for the magazine, visited the underground headquarters of a CCTV control center in London, he was astonished to find himself in "what can only be described as a bunker of spies." A team of operators controlled 160 cameras, using video-game-style joysticks to swivel the cameras and zoom in on such sights as a young man and woman talking in Leicester Square.

How did the operators feel about their surveillance powers? "The way I see it," said the man who demonstrated the system to O'Neill, "if you have nothing to hide, you have nothing to worry about." He also reported that since 2002 the center had recorded more than 24,000 incidents of misbehavior, from tipping over garbage cans to robbery and drug dealing, and that representatives from the governments or police forces of more than thirty countries had visited the center because they were considering adopting similar equipment. The CCTV system made O'Neill think of the nightmare of continuous surveillance that George Orwell portrayed in *1984*, but many people feel differently. Surveys have shown that more members of the British public accept CCTV than oppose it. Peter Fry, director of an association for institutions that use CCTV, told O'Neill, "People see these cameras as a kind of benevolent father, rather than as Big Brother."

Will CCTV stop terrorism? It would be hard for CCTV to prevent an incident like the 9/11 attacks. Operators would have to see and recognize the perpetrators in time to halt the attack. This would require a complete database of possible terror suspects, as well as accurate facial recognition software. And while CCTV could show someone planting a bomb in a trash can, possibly giving authorities a chance to keep the bomb from exploding, there might be little or nothing that the cameras could do to halt a determined suicide bomber. Two bombing attacks in 2005 showed Britons the weaknesses and the strengths of CCTV as an antiterrorism tool. On July 7, London was shaken by a coordinated series of suicide bombings in subways and elsewhere. Although video monitoring had not prevented the attack, CCTV images helped authorities determine what had happened and identify the bombers, who perished in the blasts. Two weeks later, a second round of attacks failed because the bombs did not explode. In this case, four suspects survived and fled. CCTV footage of the suspects, released to the public, contributed to their identification and arrest by police.

If CCTV cannot halt terrorist attacks, at least it aids in their investigation. Many observers, however, feel that the primary goal of CCTV is to deter ordinary crime. "The real reason cameras are deployed," says the ACLU, "is to reduce much pettier crimes, such as auto break-ins."

Does CCTV reduce crime? The evidence is unclear, and there are strong feelings on both sides. Some early studies showed crime rates falling in British cities or neighborhoods that had adopted CCTV. However, studies conducted for the British government in 2002 and 2005 failed to show much benefit. In one study, criminologists from the University of Leicester examined fourteen CCTV systems across the country. They reported in 2005 that only one area showed a drop in crime rates that could be linked to the use of CCTV. Martin Gill, a professor of criminology, said, "For supporters of CCTV, these results are disappointing. For the most part CCTV did not produce reductions in crime and it did not make people feel safer."

And camera surveillance has limits. People in some areas are worrying about the rise in street crime by gangs of young people who use the large hoods of jackets or sweatshirts to hide their faces from the cameras. Britain has spent billions of pounds (much of it taxpayer money) on its CCTV network. Even if the country stopped installing new cameras today, maintaining and operating the existing systems—which must be fully staffed every day, around the clock, to be most useful—is tremendously costly. Some critics have suggested that the minimal benefits from CCTV are not worth the high cost.

Is CCTV the future of America? Privacy advocates hope not. According to the ACLU, the lack of proven anti-crime or antiterror effectiveness is not the only reason to be wary of expanding video surveillance into new aspects of public life. CCTV, like any kind of surveillance or database, is vulnerable to abuse. Studies in Britain have revealed racial bias, for example. Camera operators give disproportionate attention to people of color. Male operators have also been caught tracking women and girls for reasons unconnected with security. Another problem with video surveillance is the lack of clear, enforceable laws to govern how such systems, and the quantities of information they gather, may be used.

Most disturbing to some critics of CCTV, though, is what they call the "chilling effect" on public life. If cameras are always watching—not just in sensitive areas such as banks and courthouses but along ordinary streets and above park benches—will people feel pressure to conform to some expected social norm? Will they worry that any distinctive clothing or unusual act is going to draw the attention of unseen observers? Will they wonder who is looking at the title of the book they're reading? Will they trust the watchers to be competent and follow the rules?

John Major, prime minister of Great Britain from 1990 to 1997, oversaw the start of the CCTV expansion. One of his most successful campaign slogans was, "If you've got nothing to hide, you've got nothing to fear." Many Americans echo that sentiment, feeling that public video surveillance is not only necessary but also harmless and desirable. Others regard it as an invasion of privacy that has not proven its worth and may permanently change the nature of American life. Perhaps the answer lies in using video surveillance thoughtfully, with public debate, and in the ways that are most likely to yield significant benefits. The majority of the public might agree, for example, that video monitoring of all playgrounds is a worthy step toward preventing child abuse and kidnapping, but that monitoring of all public parks is needlessly intrusive.

5

Students, Schools, and Safety

At school, the word *security* doesn't usually refer to the danger of international terrorism. It's more likely to mean preventing the tragedy of another school shooting or ending disruptive behavior such as drug use, fighting, and bullying. With the need to safeguard students and maintain an orderly learning environment for all, how much privacy can students be allowed? Where is the line between a young person's right to freedom of expression and a school's right to control what is said in hallways and classrooms?

Young people have constitutional rights, but some of their rights are more limited than those of adults. The law has always recognized that young people are controlled by their parents in many ways until they "come of age" and are legally considered adults. The law has also held that schools, like parents, have the legal right to place some limits on young people's freedoms.

Private schools have almost unlimited power to say what students may and may not do at school. Public schools, which are government institutions, are different.

Their control over students is governed by two basic principles. A series of court cases have defined how far schools and students can go in testing each other's limits.

The principle of *in loco parentis* is one basis for schools' authority. The Latin phrase means "in place of the parent" and refers to the fact that, while students are at school, the school stands in the role of substitute parent, responsible for making decisions in the best interests of students' welfare. A second principle has to do with the primary purpose of schools, which is education. If something that a student says or does can be shown to interfere with that educational mission, the school usually has the right to ban the behavior.

Students and the First Amendment

The idea that students have civil rights first came before the Supreme Court in 1943 in the case of *West Virginia State Board of Education* v. *Barnette*. A West Virginia law required students to recite the Pledge of Allegiance each day. Several families claimed that their children could not do so for religious reasons. When the case reached the Supreme Court, the Court ruled that the students were protected by the First Amendment to the Constitution, which grants freedom of religion, speech, the press, and assembly. The Court overturned the law that required all students to recite the pledge.

Twenty-five years later the Court was again asked to rule on the question of students' First Amendment rights. The case of *Tinker* v. *Des Moines Independent School District* was argued in 1968, when the United States was at war in Vietnam. Among the many Americans who opposed that war were three Iowa students, ages thirteen, fifteen, and sixteen, who wore black armbands to school as

SIBLINGS MARY BETH AND JOHN TINKER, IN 1968, DISPLAY THE
ARMBANDS THEY WORE TO SCHOOL TO MOURN THOSE KILLED IN THE
VIETNAM WAR. THE ARMBAND CASE REACHED THE SUPREME COURT
AND TESTED THE LIMITS OF YOUNG PEOPLE'S FREEDOM OF EXPRES-
SION IN SCHOOL.

symbols of protest. The school suspended the students, who, along with their families, fought the suspensions all the way to the Supreme Court, claiming that the students' free-speech rights had been violated.

In deciding the *Tinker* case in 1969, the Court focused on whether the speech in question had disrupted education, created disorder, or invaded others' rights. It decided that the armbands had done none of these things. In handing down the Court's ruling in favor of the students, Justice Abe Fortas wrote:

> **It can hardly be argued that either students or teachers shed their constitutional rights to freedom of speech or expression at the schoolhouse gate. . . . School officials do not possess absolute authority over their students. Students in school as well as out of school are "persons" under our Constitution. They are possessed of fundamental rights which the State must respect. . . . In the absence of specific showing of constitutionally valid reasons to regulate their speech, students are entitled to freedom of expression of their views.**

Tinker was a victory for student rights. In the 1986 case of *Bethel School District v. Fraser*, however, the Court decided that a school board had the right to suspend a student who had used crude language in a speech at a school assembly. The Court's point was that although adults cannot be prohibited from using offensive language, students can, because their rights are more limited than those of adults.

Two years later another First Amendment case, *Hazelwood School v. Kuhlmeier* (1988), focused on censorship. The case involved two articles written by students for a high school newspaper in Missouri. One article dealt with student pregnancies; the other was about students with divorced parents. The school censored both articles, refusing to allow them to be printed in the school newspaper. The students sued. The Supreme Court ruled that the school had the right to censor speech in the school newspaper because the paper, unlike the black armbands in the *Tinker* case, represented the entire school, not the opinions of individuals.

In March 2007 the U.S. Court of Appeals heard arguments in *Morse* v. *Frederick*, a free-speech case with a different twist. The speech in question was a banner, and the incident took place outside school property. In 2002, when the Olympic torch was carried through Juneau, Alaska, a student who had not attended school that day stood on the public sidewalk across the street from his school and held up a banner reading "Bong Hits 4 Jesus." The principal crossed the street and pulled down the banner. The school suspended the student for ten days because of the content of his message, which it claimed promoted illegal drug use.

When the student sued the school, the court ruled in the student's favor. Its decision was that the school had no right to censor or punish the student's speech. The banner, said the court, had not disrupted educational activity. The school then appealed this decision to the Supreme Court. Students, parents, school administrators, and free speech advocates are waiting with great interest to learn the Court's ruling in *Frederick* v. *Morse* because that decision in the case is expected to influence schools' rights to control what students say in other locations outside school, such as Web pages.

Another form of student self-expression came under scrutiny in 2007 in Rhode Island. At issue was the question of how medieval your yearbook photo can be. A school planned to censor the photograph of Patrick Agin, a seventeen-year-old student who belonged to an organization that studied and reenacted medieval history. Agin had posed for his picture wearing a medieval costume. His fake sword, said the school, violated the "zero tolerance" weapons policy. The ACLU filed suit on Agin's behalf, pointing out that the school's own mascot, a Revolutionary War soldier, was often pictured with weapons, and that other sections of the yearbook showed students posing with toy guns and a knife. Under those circumstances, excluding a photo that reflected a student's deep interest in medieval history was "unreasonable and arbitrary." The state board of education agreed with the ACLU and ordered the school to publish Agin's photo, chain mail and all.

Students and the Fourth Amendment

The Fourth Amendment protects Americans from unreasonable searches and seizures. Does this mean your school can't require you to walk through a metal detector? No. Given the risk of guns and knives being carried into schools, the courts have held that metal-detection screening is reasonable in schools, as it is in airports, courthouses, and many other public places. Teachers and principals also have the right to search your locker whenever they want, because lockers are school property. Purses, backpacks, and other items of student property are another, more complicated, story.

The standard for searching students' belongings was set by the 1985 Supreme Court case *New Jersey* v. *T.L.O.* After a teacher found two high school girls smoking, one student confessed and was suspended for three days. The second denied that she had smoked, so the vice principal searched her purse. In addition to cigarettes, the search turned up marijuana. The student was suspended and

METAL DETECTORS AND OTHER SECURITY CHECKS AREN'T JUST FOR AIRPORTS ANY MORE. FOR SOME STUDENTS, THE SCHOOL DAY BEGINS WITH A SEARCH FOR PROHIBITED ITEMS SUCH AS WEAPONS.

charged as a delinquent. Her parents sued, claiming that the vice principal had violated the girl's rights by searching her purse without a warrant.

The Supreme Court decided in favor of the school. Its

ruling in *New Jersey* v. *T.L.O.* set forth the standards for school searches of student property. Students' Fourth Amendment rights, declared the Court, are more restricted than those of adults. School officials may search student property without warrants. The schools' right to search is not unlimited, however. Searches can be carried out only when the school has reasonable suspicion that the search will reveal evidence that the student is breaking either a school rule or a law. In addition, the search must be reasonable in scope—students cannot be asked to undress for a search, for example, unless they are reasonably suspected of hiding drugs beneath their clothing.

Drug testing is another area in which students, schools, and courts have debated the Fourth Amendment's protection. The cases in question are not those in which the schools can show that there was reason to suspect that a particular student had been using drugs. The controversy concerns what the ACLU and other privacy advocates have called "suspicionless testing"—making drug testing mandatory for all students, or choosing students at random to undergo testing, without any link to suspicion of actual drug abuse.

The subject started to become a constitutional matter in the early 1990s. School officials in the small rural town of Vernonia, Oregon, became convinced that high school athletes were a big part of what they saw as the town's growing drug problem. They ordered that anyone who wanted to participate in school sports had to be tested for drugs. This meant producing urine samples in the presence of adult supervisors. Refusal to take the test meant suspension from sports for two seasons.

One athlete felt he should not have to be tested. No one, after all, could point to any reason to think that he was a drug user. His parents sued the school on his behalf, claiming that the testing policy was a violation of his

A DOG IS BEING TRAINED TO SNIFF SCHOOL LOCKERS FOR
MARIJUANA, COCAINE, AND OTHER ILLEGAL DRUGS. AS SCHOOL
PROPERTY, LOCKERS MAY BE SEARCHED AT ANY TIME. TESTING
STUDENTS THEMSELVES FOR DRUGS IS MORE CONTROVERSIAL.

privacy and his right to be free of unreasonable searches. The case, *Vernonia School District* v. *Acton*, was heard by the Supreme Court in 1995. The Court upheld the school's policy, ruling that constitutional rights may be interpreted differently in schools from other places. The school had a clear interest in preventing drug use, said the Court, and in addition athletes have lower expectations of personal privacy than nonathletes, because they are used to communal showers and locker rooms.

Vernonia and similar decisions support the legality of the drug-testing programs that are currently in force in about a thousand middle schools and high schools across the United States. Such programs affect students who take part in extracurricular activities—not just sports, but clubs and other activities that take place outside the classroom but under the supervision of the school. Some states or school districts also test students who drive to school; the courts have upheld this use of drug testing. Most programs are random, testing a few students at a time rather than trying to test every student.

Will drug testing be coming soon to your school, if it's not there already? The federal government provides funding for some of the existing student drug-testing programs and wants to bring testing to more schools. The Office of National Drug Control Policy (ONDCP) is committed to reducing drug abuse among young people and believes that random testing is an effective way to do so. One model for student testing programs is the military's policy of conducting random drug tests. Over a twenty-year period of military drug testing, the percentage of positive tests (indicating drug use) fell from 27 percent to 1.5 percent. Yet the Drug Policy Alliance, which opposes student testing, points out that two 2003 studies of student drug use—one of which involved 94,000 students in 900 schools—showed no difference in drug use between schools with testing programs and those without them.

Aside from effectiveness, some privacy advocates question whether students' test results are kept confidential. Others fear that the tests, which are sometimes reviewed by outside labs and sometimes handled by school staff alone, are not always competently administered, which could lead to false positive tests that might unfairly brand a student as a drug user. Supporters of drug testing feel that although such risks exist, the benefits of drug testing outweigh them. "I think the far greater risk is using the drug that can have adverse consequences on brain, body and behavior," says Dr. Bertha Madras of the ONDCP. Madras points out that under the law, students have different expectations of privacy from adults, and that student privacy should not be allowed to override health and safety concerns. She says, "I think that privacy issues are really interesting for adolescents. If a child is doing something that is illegal, then how do we weigh the more important value, which is how to protect a child? Really, ask yourself logically, do you feel young people who don't have a fully developed sense of self should be able to do things that are illegal to harm themselves."

Existing drug-testing programs involve students who take part in extracurricular activities. In a few cases, states or school districts have wanted to extend drug testing to *all* students. These plans have faced strict legal scrutiny because of the difference between voluntary and enforced participation. Students who voluntarily join extracurricular programs can choose not to participate if they object to the drug testing, but classroom attendance is mandatory for all, and the idea of forcing every kid to be tested for drugs is unacceptable to many people. So far all of the proposed plans have been struck down as violations of privacy. In 2001, for example, a Texas school district lost a lawsuit in its battle to make drug tests mandatory for all students in grades seven through twelve. Supporters of drug testing, though, say that the fight is not over. To some of them, stamping out drug use is as important a security issue as fighting terrorism.

Online Rights and Wrongs

When students go online, they enter a dazzling world of entertainment choices and communication possibilities. Depending upon where they go and what they do while online, they may also enter a legal gray area. The issue is schools' rights to control what kids post on the Internet, even from their home computers.

In 2006 seven high school students were suspended for five days in Parsippany, New Jersey, after they created two accounts on MySpace.com and posted pictures of fellow students and teachers that they had taken at school with their cell phones. The photos were ornamented with vulgar and humorous statements, but, according to school superintendent James Dwyer, the problem wasn't the content of the commentary—it was the fact that the students had used photos of other people without their permission. Dwyer speculated that posting pictures of other kids, in particular, might be a legal issue because the kids' parents hadn't given permission for the photographs to be published.

Students have won some battles for online freedom of expression. A school district in Washington State agreed in 2006 to pay $62,000 in damages to a young man who had been expelled from school for creating a Web site that mocked a school official with raunchy images. A court found that the Web site had not disrupted school operations and had not been created with school resources; the student's right to free expression had therefore been violated. A related case involved a New Jersey eighth grader who criticized his school on his Web site, was punished, and sued the school. That case cost the school district more than $117,000 in damages.

In 2001, after a Florida high school student was suspended for ten days for creating a Web site that was critical of his school, the American Civil Liberties Union (ACLU) got involved—and got him back in school after four days. The ACLU also negotiated an agreement with a Colorado high school that suspended a student for fifteen days in 2006, after he posted critical comments about the school on MySpace. Speaking for the ACLU, attorney Hugo Gottschalk said, "School authorities do not have the right to impose discipline for statements that students make off campus." Not everyone agrees. A Florida teacher is suing a student for posting crude sexual comments next to her picture on a Web site. When she came across the picture and comments, she felt degraded and humiliated. "The teacher was maligned by this kid," says her lawyer.

Some guidelines are clear. Just as with speech in other settings, Internet speech can be considered criminal if it contains threats of violence or libelous (untrue and demeaning) statements. Most of the time, personal opinions fall into the category of protected speech. But between these two extremes lies the uncharted territory of rumors, bullying, parody, and vulgarity—uses of the Internet that might be tasteless or hurtful, but are not necessarily illegal. Should schools be allowed to discipline students for them?

The courts have already established the right of schools to discipline kids for expressions that take place in school and disrupt school operations, and the right of schools to censor school publications. But what about private blogs or Web pages made outside school? A 2005 study found that 19 percent of teenagers with access to the Internet kept a blog, and that 38 percent of teens read blogs, and the percentage of students who blog or maintain personal Web pages is growing every day. Several court decisions have held that viewing such materials at school, or even talking about them there, may be considered a disruption of education, which can be punished. For many school administrators and victims of cyberbullying, though, the trouble comes from what students view on their own time. Internet providers, or the owners of sites such as MySpace, often shut down Web pages when schools and parents complain. But not until the Supreme Court issues a ruling on students' off-campus rights of expression will there be anything approaching a universal standard for evaluating students' online speech.

Cyberbullying is a growing problem. Students use their personal blogs or Web pages on sites such as MySpace or Facebook to criticize, gossip about, or attack other students. As a result, most schools have blocked access to these popular sites from computers at school. That doesn't solve the problem of postings made from, and seen on, home computers. In some ways, its victims say, it is worse than real-life bullying.

Unlike real-life bullying, which is witnessed by whomever happens to be in a school hallway or lunchroom at a given moment, cyberbullying may occur in front of online communities that can be huge. And it is often anonymous, as one ninth-grade girl reports: "Whenever I was on my computer, I'd get IMs saying that everyone hated me and I should watch my back. It seemed like it was from girls who I thought were my friends. When I confronted them, they denied it and blamed it on someone else. I never knew who was really behind it. I got really paranoid and couldn't concentrate in school." Some cases of cyberbullying have included lewd or graphic insults.

Such cases are head-on collisions between young people's right to express themselves freely and the duty of parents, schools, and society in general to regulate their behavior. Although some argue that schools have no right to censor a student's off-campus expression, many teachers, parents, and kids who've been harassed online have a different view. They feel that part of a school's educational mission is to create a community whose members respect each other beyond the classroom.

6
Privacy and Security in the Future

Your ideas about privacy may not be the same as your parents' or grandparents'. Different generations of Americans have different overall expectations about what privacy means, reports David H. Holtzman in *Privacy Lost: How Technology Is Endangering Your Privacy* (2006). Those changing attitudes will shape society's decisions about security and privacy in the future.

Older Americans, according to Holtzman's research, have high expectations of personal privacy. Many of them are used to dealing with people face-to-face or over the telephone; they are less familiar with shopping or conducting business online, and some never do it at all. They expect government and businesses to safeguard their personal information and feel that information leaks, or unauthorized uses of information, are betrayals of trust. Their main fears about privacy violations concern identity theft and financial losses.

Privacy expectations are lower among the young, who grew up in the era of reality TV, Webcams and videocams, downloading and uploading, networking and multitasking, blogging, texting, and IMing. "They know that their gadgets are two-way," says Holtzman. "It's natural for them to believe that everyone's watching. To them, there's no such thing as privacy." This view may be a little—or a lot—exaggerated. But it's a good thing that younger Americans are at home with high technology, because security, privacy, and technology are ever more closely intertwined.

Intrusive technology and information-gathering are not necessarily evil, in the opinion of David Brin, a scientist and science-fiction writer. In his 1998 nonfiction book *The Transparent Society*, Brin claimed that the rise of digital information storage, video monitoring, and other new technologies means that centralized databases of information about everyone are bound to exist, and that authorities are bound to use them. Instead of trying to fight the inevitable or screen themselves from scrutiny, citizens should insist that the authorities submit to the same scrutiny, or to an even stricter degree of oversight from independent inspectors chosen by the people. Brin's idea is that if the public knows what information the government or other entities have gathered, and how they are using it, there will be less anxiety about Big Brother. If the authorities watch us, in other words, we should be able to watch them. "We can stand living exposed to scrutiny, if in return we get flashlights of our own that we can shine on anyone who might do us harm," Brin says.

In the wake of 9/11, Brin argued that the conflict between security and privacy was a false one, with advocates on both sides "screaming like pro wrestlers" and making people believe they had to choose between safety and freedom. In reality, he believes, the key is to focus on protecting the data that can cause harm, such as medical records, and not to worry about the fact that public databases might reveal your favorite brand of salad dressing or the books you bought online last year. If Brin is right, we

A U.S. SOLDIER IN RAMADI, IRAQ, SCANS THE IRIS OF A MAN WHO HAS VOLUNTEERED TO JOIN THE IRAQI ARMY. UNIQUE PATTERNS IN THE COLORED PART OF THE EYE ARE INCREASINGLY USED FOR IDENTIFICATION AND SECURITY PURPOSES—PART OF THE GROWING FIELD OF BIOMETRICS.

should resign ourselves to losing control over a lot of personal information, while fighting for the responsible use of the information that really matters.

Coming Soon (or Already Here)

Intelligence and law enforcement agencies have a strong interest in tools that can help track people or information.

Some of those tools have already arrived and are finding new applications all the time. Others are just over the horizon.

Global positioning systems (GPS) use Earth-orbiting satellites to pinpoint the exact locations of GPS devices anywhere on Earth. Those devices now come in the form of microchips that can be installed in cell phones and cars and even implanted under people's skin. Car rental companies, insurance companies, and police departments are already using them to track and find missing vehicles (and parents are using them to see where their kids go in their cars). Some sex offenders have been implanted with chips so that authorities can locate them at any time, and there have been calls to put chips in other violent criminals. Is it a stretch of the imagination to think that all criminals might someday be implanted? What about all suspects? What about all citizens? Universal GPS chips would help police find missing children—but they would also let the government know exactly where everyone is, all the time. Is that an acceptable trade-off? At some point Americans may find themselves weighing that question.

Radio frequency identification devices (RFIDs) are chips that use short-wave radio signals to broadcast distinctive codes over distances that range from about twenty feet to several hundred feet. Small and increasingly cheap to manufacture, RFIDs are already being used in business. Taking inventory in an auto-parts warehouse, for example, is a lot faster and easier if every item in the warehouse is tagged with an RFID. Instead of having to move and count all the engines and batteries, workers just have to walk up and down the aisles with readers that collect the RFID information and send it to a computer.

You may already have bought a pair of shoes or a DVD with an RFID embedded in it. Someday everything you own or use may contain these tiny identifiers. If you paid for the objects with a credit card, check, or bank

IF THIS DOG GETS LOST, A SECURITY SERVICE CAN USE A GLOBAL SATELLITE NETWORK TO PINPOINT ITS LOCATION—OR AT LEAST THE LOCATION OF THE GPS UNIT ATTACHED TO ITS HARNESS. PEOPLE CAN BE TRACKED THE SAME WAY, WITH IMPLANTED DEVICES THAT CANNOT EASILY BE REMOVED. IS THIS A BOON TO SECURITY OR THE END OF PRIVACY?

account, they'll be linked to your name and other information. The RFIDs are encoded, so no one would be able to walk past your home and scan its contents without the correct readers—but someday data aggregators may pool RFID tag information the way they now pool lists of grocery purchases. Embedded in driver's licenses, RFIDs could be used to encode security rankings like those planned for the ill-fated CAPPS II passenger screening program. Would this mean that dangerous people would be kept out of places that are vulnerable to terrorism, or would it mean that the government would install RFID trackers everywhere, like Britain's video surveillance cameras, to track all of us as we go about our daily business?

Would you have a chip put into your body to save yourself the trouble of waiting in line at a night club? In 2004 a club in Barcelona, Spain, offered patrons the chance to buy an RFID chip that, once implanted, lets them pass through club doors without waiting in line. The chip is coded to identify members to the club's RFID readers. RFID implants may also be used in place of identification cards for people who have to pass through security checkpoints every day, such as employees of military bases and government buildings. An RFID chip could even replace a passport, becoming a permanent, personal identification card. Unless the information on the card is encrypted, however, and access to the card-readers is strictly controlled, the information could be stolen or misused by anyone with a reader.

Biometric data is coming into use in driver's licenses and ID cards. Biometrics is the sophisticated use of measuring physical features to identify people. Applications now in use include scans of the iris of the eye, which has patterns that are believed to be as distinctive as a fingerprint, and software programs that recognize faces (poorly, as some studies of their effectiveness have shown, but they are improving all the time). Now being researched are chips that can immediately identify people from DNA traces such as handprints and fallen hairs.

Identification is likely to remain a central issue of the debate over security and privacy. One question is whether citizens of the United States should be issued—and required to carry—a national ID card. Those who argue for such a card claim that it would make identification theft more difficult by giving everyone a single, unique ID tag. It would replace the more than two hundred documents currently being used as ID, including drivers' licenses issued under different systems and levels of protection, with a single standard. It would make it easier for security officials to know who crosses the national border.

Opponents of national ID cards range from the far left to the far right. Liberal organizations such as the ACLU think that national IDs could be too easily misused to track the population; so do conservatives such as Phyllis Schlafly of the Eagle Forum. To many the idea of a national ID is reminiscent of totalitarian states such as Nazi Germany or the Soviet Union, where people were required to produce their "papers" upon demand by any official. The effectiveness of a national ID has also been questioned. The ID would likely be based upon documents such as birth certificates and Social Security cards, but decades of identity theft have shown how vulnerable these are to forgery. Nor is it clear that national ID cards would stop terrorism. Several of the 9/11 hijackers had Social Security numbers and valid driver's licenses.

In 2005 President George W. Bush signed the Real ID Act, which, if accepted by all the states, would turn driver's licenses into national ID cards, readable by RFID scanners, under the oversight of the Department of Homeland Security. Critics such as the ACLU have argued that the project, with administrative costs estimated at between

Stolen Identities

Everyone has heard horror stories about identity theft. Take the case of the Oklahoma man who tried to rent a tuxedo for his sister's wedding, only to have the store reject his credit card. He didn't know why the card was rejected, so he checked with the credit-card company. That's when he learned that his identity had been stolen. Another man had used it to buy an apartment building in New York, rent cars, purchase expensive furs and jewelry, and even operate an escort service. All at once that Oklahoma man found himself half a million dollars in debt. It took him two years of constant effort to untangle the mess and restore his good name and credit.

Identity theft in the United States falls under the jurisdiction of the Federal Trade Commission (FTC). In 2005 a total of 255,565 cases of identity theft were reported to the FTC. Nearly a third of the victims were between eighteen and twenty-nine years old, and 5 percent of victims were under the age of eighteen.

Anyone who has a Social Security number, a job, a bank account, credit card, or cell phone account in his or her own name is vulnerable to ID theft. And thieves don't target only the wealthy—they will use any personal or financial information they can get their hands on to try to open new accounts in someone else's name. To protect yourself, the FTC recommends that you destroy personal and financial documents, such as credit card invoices and old prescription bottles, instead of throwing them in the trash. If you shop online, consider setting up a free account with a secure third-party payer, such as Paypal, instead of using your credit card number for each purchase. You can find other tips on reducing your risk of identity theft, safeguarding your information online, and dealing with identity theft at the FTC Web site:

http://www.ftc.gov/bcp/edu/microsites/idtheft

IDENTITY THIEVES CAN MEMORIZE SOMEONE'S PIN (PERSONAL IDENTIFICATION NUMBER) WITH JUST A CASUAL GLANCE. IN THE INFORMATION ERA, PRIVATE DATA—WHETHER IT'S A PIN OR A SOCIAL SECURITY NUMBER—IS AS VALUABLE AS MONEY.

$11 and $23 billion dollars, would have a destructive effect on privacy while offering little real protection against terrorism. In January 2007 Maine's state legislature voted not to accept Real ID, and similar votes were pending in other states. It is unclear how, or whether, the Real ID program will work without the compliance of all fifty states.

A Middle Way?

People who have strong feelings about either national security or personal privacy are likely also to have strong feelings about the motives of those who disagree with them. This is probably a mistake. Calling for strong protections of civil liberties and privacy, either before 9/11 or after, is not the same thing as wanting to hand the country over to its enemies. Nor is wanting to do whatever is needed to fight terrorism the same thing as wanting to turn America into a police state or trample on privacy.

Can security and privacy coexist? They can, but keeping them in balance requires everyone, ordinary people as well as policymakers, to think about the issues and make informed decisions. In Washington, D.C., in 2003, at a conference on the use of technology in Homeland Security operations, James Gilmore, a former governor of Virginia and chairman of the National Advisory Commission on Terrorism, said, "I believe that as citizens we have an obligation to try to put together both security and freedom at the same time."

The reality is that Americans—and all people—live in a world where security faces new and unpredictable challenges. To survive those challenges people with opposing views may have to meet somewhere in the middle. Perhaps such a meeting of the minds might resemble the feeling of unity that swept the United States in the wake of the terrorist attacks of 2001. Differences temporarily forgotten,

Americans from all points of the political compass showed themselves to be capable of generosity, patriotism, and goodwill. Those qualities should help the nation agree to seek out the balance that best preserves both security and privacy, while remaining always aware of potential threats to both.

Notes

Chapter 1

p. 9, par. 2, Dennis Cauchon, "For Many on September 11, Survival Was No Accident." *USA Today*, December 20, 2001, http://www.usatoday.com/news/sept11/2001/12/19/usatcov-wtcsurvival.htm

p. 9, par. 3, Cauchon.

p. 10, par. 3, Barbara Kantrowitz, et al. "Generation 9–11." *Newsweek*, November 12, 2001, Vol. 138, Issue 20, pp. 46–55, http://search.ebscohost.com/login.aspx?direct=true&db=f5h&AN=5457456&loginpage=reflogin.asp&site=ehost-live

p. 11, par. 1, Phil Hirschkorn, "9/11 Jurors Face Complex Life-or-Death Decisions." *CNN.com*, April 26, 2006. http://www.cnn.com/2006/LAW/04/25/moussaoui.trial/

pp. 14–16, Transcript of President Bush's September 20, 2001, address from http://archives.cnn.com/2001/US/09/20/gen.bush.transcript

p. 18, par. 2, John Ashcroft, "A Clear and Present Danger." In Amitai Etzioni and Jason Marsh, eds. *Rights vs. Public Safety After 9/11*, Lanham, MD: Rowman & Littlefield, 2003, pp. 4–5.

p. 18, par. 2–p. 19, par. 1, "The Privacy Office of the U.S. Department of Homeland Security." http://www.dhs.gov/xabout/structure/editorial_0338.shtm

p. 19, par. 1–p. 20, par. 1, Aryeh Neier, "Lost Liberties: Ashcroft and the Assault on Personal Freedom." In M. Katherine B. Darmer et al., eds., *Civil Liberties vs. National Security in a Post-9/11 World*. Amherst, NY: Prometheus Books, 2004, pp. 34–35.

p. 20, par. 2, Heather MacDonald, "Straight Talk on Homeland Security." *City Journal*, Summer 2003. http://www.city-journal.org/html/13_3_straight_talk.html

p. 21, par. 3, Linda Greenhouse, "In New York Visit, O'Connor Foresees Limits on Freedom." *New York Times*, September 29, 2001, p. B5.

Chapter 2

p. 25, par. 2, Cited in David H. Holtzman, *Privacy Lost: How Technology Is Endangering Your Privacy*. San Francisco: Jossey-Bass, 2006, p. 93.

p. 28, par. 1, Benjamin Franklin (attributed), *An Historical Review of the Constitution and Government of Pennsylvania*, London, 1759, http://www.futureofthebook.com/stories/storyReader$605

p. 29, par. 2, Franklin's letter to Hume cited in Jared Sparks, *Life of Benjamin Franklin, 1836–1840*, http://www.ushistory.org/franklin/biography/chap01.htm

p. 29, par. 3–p. 30, par. 1, David Hume, *An Enquiry Concerning the Principles of Morals*, Section III, Of Justice, Part I, http://etext.library.adelaide.edu.au/h/hume/david/h92pm/chapter3.htm

p. 34, par. 3–p. 35, par. 1, Samuel Warren and Louis Brandeis, "The Right to Privacy." *Harvard Law Review*, Vol. IV, No. 5, December 15, 1890, http://faculty.uml.edu/sgallagher/Brandeisprivacy.htm

p. 35, par. 2, Brian Coe and Paul Gates. *The Snapshot Photograph: The Rise of Popular Photography, 1888–1989*, London: Ash and Grant, 1977, p. 18.

p. 36, par. 1, Warren and Brandeis.

Chapter 3

p. 47, pars. 2–3, John Ashcroft, "A Clear and Present Danger." In Amitai Etzioni and Jason Marsh, eds., *Rights vs. Public*

Safety After 9/11. Lanham, MD: Rowman & Littlefield, 2003, pp. 3, 8.

p. 47, par. 4, Quoted in Aryeh Neier, "Lost Liberties: Ashcroft and the Assault on Personal Freedom." In M. Katherine B. Darmer et al., eds., *Civil Liberties vs. National Security in a Post-9/11 World*. Amherst, NY: Prometheus Books, 2004, pp. 39–40.

p. 48, par. 2, Darren W. Davis and Brian B. Silver. "Civil Liberties vs. Security: Public Opinion in the Context of the Terrorist Attacks on America. *American Journal of Political Science*. Vol. 48, No. 1, January 2004, pp. 28–46.

p. 49, par. 1, Peter M. Thomson, "White Paper on the USA Patriot Act's 'Roving' Electronic Surveillance Amendment to the Foreign Intelligence Surveillance Act." Federalist Society for Law and Public Policy Studies. Reprinted in Jamuna Carroll, ed., *Privacy*. Detroit: Greenhaven Press, 2006, p. 39.

p. 49, par. 2, David Cole, "Let's Fight Terrorism, Not the Constitution," in Amitai Etzioni and Jason Marsh, editors, *Rights vs. Public Safety After 9/11*, Lanham, MD: Rowman & Littlefield, 2003, pp. 35, 42.

p. 50, par. 2, "Feds Give Stats on Snooping." May 21, 2003. *CBS News*. http://www.cbsnews.com/stories/2003/05/21/national/main554924.shtml

p. 50, par. 3, "Rebel Librarians Go on a Tear." May 28, 2003. *CBS News*. http://www.cbsnews.com/stories/2003/05/28/national/main555885.shtml

p. 56, par. 1–p. 57, par. 1, David Sarasohn, "The Problems to Come for the Patriot Act." *Oregonian*, December 3, 2006, p. D2.

p. 58, par. 3, Hady Omar story from "Guilty Until Proven: Three 9/11 Detainees Tell Their Story." *CBS News*, August 24, 2003, at http://www.cbsnews.com/stories/2003/04/06/60minutes/main548023.shtml

p. 59, par. 2, Nacer Mustafa story from Anthony Lewis. "First They Came for the Muslims. . . ." In *The American Prospect*, March 1, 2003. http://www.prospect.org/print/V14/3/lewis-a.html, and Dale Lezon, "Truth Set Ex-Detainees Free in Terrorism Probe." Houston Chronicle, January 27, 2002. http://www.chron.com/disp/story.mpl/special/terror/front/1227383.html

p. 66, par. 1, "Scott Pelley Reports on the CIA's Rendition Pro-

gram." March 6, 2005. http://www.cbsnews.com/stories/
2005/03/04/60minutes/main678155.shtml

p. 66, par. 2, Jay S. Bybee, "Memorandum for Alberto R. Gonzales." In M. Katherine B. Darmer et al., eds., *Civil Liberties vs. National Security in a Post-9/11 World.* Amherst,
NY: Prometheus Books, 2004, p. 306.

p. 69, par. 1, American Civil Liberties Union, "The Patriot Act:
Where It Stands." http://action.aclu.org/reformthepatrio-
tact/whereitstands.html

p. 69, par. 1, President George W. Bush, March 9, 2006, Department of Justice Web site. http://www.lifeandliberty
.gov/

Chapter 4

p. 78, par. 1, *Kyllo* v. *United States.* In M. Katherine B. Darmer
et al., eds., *Civil Liberties vs. National Security in a Post-
9/11 World.* Amherst, NY: Prometheus Books, 2004,
p. 81.

p. 80, par. 3, Electronic Privacy Information Center, "Secure
Flight." http://www.epic.org/privacy/airtravel/secureflight.
html

p. 80, par. 3, Electronic Privacy Information Center, "Passenger Profiling." http://www.epic.org/privacy/airtravel/
profiling.html

p. 82, par. 3, David H. Holtzman, *Privacy Lost: How Technology Is Endangering Your Privacy.* San Francisco: Jossey-
Bass, 2006, p. 199.

p. 83, par. 2, Holtzman, p. 192.

p. 83, par. 3, David Colker and Joseph Menn, "ChoicePoint
Had Earlier Data Leak." *South Florida Sun-Sentinel.*
March 4, 2005. http://www.sun-sentinel.com/business/
local/balchoicept0302,0,5194720.story?coll=sfla-
business-headlines

p. 83, par. 4, Holtzman, p. 194.

p. 86, par. 2, Center for Democracy and Technology, "Mandatory Data Retention—Invasive, Risky, Unnecessary, Inef-
fective." June 6, 2006. http://www.cdt.org/security/

p. 87, par. 2, Stephanie Amour, "Companies Keep an Eye on
Workers' Internet Use." *USA Today*, February 20, 2006.
http://www. usatoday.com/tech/news/internetprivacy/2006
-02-20-internet-abuse_x.htm

p. 88, par. 2, Gus Arroyo, "The Impact of Video Monitoring

Technology on Police Field Operations." *Police Futurists International.* November 22, 2002. Reprinted in Jamuna Carroll, *Privacy.* Detroit: Greenhaven Press, 2005, p. 95.

p. 90, par. 3, Brendan O'Neill, "Watching You Watching Me." *New Statesman.* October 2, 2006. http://www.newstatesman.com/200610020022

p. 92, par. 3–p. 93, par. 1, Amy Reiter, "Putting Mary Poppins Under Surveillance." *salon.com*, July 17, 2003, http://dir.salon.com/story/mwt/feature/2003/07/17/nanny_cams/index_np.html

p. 93, par. 5, Personal communication to author.

p. 94, par. 1, O'Neill.

p. 94, par. 2, O'Neill.

p. 95, par. 2, American Civil Liberties Union. "What's Wrong with Public Video Surveillance?" February 25, 2002. http://www.aclu.org/privacy/spying/14863res20020225.html

p. 95, par. 3, *BBC News*, "CCTV systems 'fail to cut crime.'" February 24, 2005. http://news.bbc.co.uk/1/hi/england/leicestershire/4294693.stm

p. 96, par. 2, American Civil Liberties Union, "What's Wrong with Public Video Surveillance?" February 25, 2002. http://www.aclu.org/privacy/spying/14863res20020225.html

p. 96, par. 3–p. 97, par. 1, Jeffrey Rosen, *The Naked Crowd: Reclaiming Security and Freedom in an Anxious Age.* New York: Random House, 2004, p. 36.

Chapter 5

p. 101, par. 2, Justice Abe Fortas, *Tinker v. Des Moines Independent School District* (393 U.S. 503, 1969). http://law.enotes.com/everyday-law-encyclopedia/student-rights-free-speech

p. 103, par. 1, American Civil Liberties Union, "Rhode Island Officials Rule School Can't Censor Teen's Yearbook Photo," January 19, 2007. http://www.aclu.org/freespeech/youth/28109prs20070119.html

p. 107, par. 2, Alexandra Gekas, "No Child Left Untested?" *Newsweek*, January 30, 2007. http://www.msnbc.msn.com/id/16893833/site/newsweek/

p. 107, par. 3–p. 108, par. 1, Gekas.

p. 108, par. 2, Gekas.

p. 108, par. 3–p. 109, par. 1, American Civil Liberties Union, "State Law Challenges to Student Drug Testing." November 12, 2005. http:// www.aclu.org/drugpolicy/testing/ 10846res20051101.html

p. 109, par. 3, National Coalition Against Censorship. http://www.ncac.org/internet/related/20061206~NJ-Parsippany~Students_suspended_myspace.cfm

p. 109, par. 4–p. 110, par. 1, Electronic Frontier Foundation,"Blogger's FAG: Student Blogging," http://www.eff. org/bloggers/lg/faq-students.php

p. 110, par. 2, Kelli Kennedy, "Not-So-My-Space Anymore." *Lakeland Ledger*, April 23, 2006, http://www.theledger. com/apps/pbcs.dll/article?AID=/20060423/NEWS/604230 392/-1/NEWS0101

p. 110, par. 2, Kennedy.

p. 111, par. 1, "Blogger's FAQ—Student Blogging." Electronic Frontier Foundation, http://www.eff.org/bloggers/lg/faq-students.php

p. 111, par. 2, Rosalind Wiseman, "Kids Are Using Technology to Hurt and Humiliate Each Other," *Parade*, February 25, 2007, http://www.parade.com/articles/editions/2007/ edition_02-5-2007/Cyberbullying

Chapter 6

p. 113, par. 1, David H. Holtzman, *Privacy Lost: How Technology Is Endangering Your Privacy*. San Francisco: Jossey-Bass, 2006, pp. 140–146.

p. 114, par. 1, Holtzman, p. 145.

p. 114, par. 2, "Special Report: New Threats to Privacy?" *BusinessWeek Online*, June 5, 2002. http://www.business-week.com/technology/content/jun2002/tc2002065_6863. htm

p. 114, par. 3, BusinessWeek Online.

p. 120, par. 1, Holtzman, p. 24.

p. 120, par. 2, Federal Trade Commission ID Theft Clearinghouse Data, January 2005–December 2005. Released January 26, 2006. http://www.consumer.gov/idtheft/pdf/ synovate_report.pdf

p. 122, par. 1, Steven Musil, "Week in Review: Got Real ID?" CNET News.com. March 2, 2007. http://news.com.com

/Week+in+review+Got+Real+ID/2100-1083_3-6163695.
html?tag=item

All Web sites were available and accurate when this book was
sent to press.

Further Information

Further Reading

Bridegam, Martha. *The Right to Privacy*. Philadelphia, PA: Chelsea House, 2003.

Carroll, Jamuna, ed. *Privacy*. Detroit, MI: Greenhaven Press, 2005.

Cothran, Helen. *National Security*. San Diego, CA: Greenhaven Press, 2004.

Etzioni, Amitai, and Jason H. Marsh, eds. *Rights vs. Public Safety after 9/11*. Lanham, MD: Rowman & Littlefield, 2003.

Fridell, Ron. *Privacy vs. Security: Your Rights in Conflict*. Berkeley Heights, NJ: Enslow, 2004.

Gottfried, Ted. *Homeland Security Versus Constitutional Rights*. Minneapolis, MN: Twenty-First Century, 2003.

Stewart, Gail. *America Under Attack: September 11, 2001*. San Diego, CA: Lucent, 2002.

Web Sites

http://www.aclu.org/
The American Civil Liberties Union (ACLU) site has a section on national security, with information on topics that include wiretapping and terrorism, and a section on privacy and technology. The ACLU focuses on safeguarding civil liberties.

http://www.dhs.gov/index.shtm
The home page of the U.S. Department of Homeland Security (DHS) offers information for citizens about DHS activities, as well as guidelines for emergency preparedness and news on security-related topics.

http://www.epic.org/
The Electronic Privacy Information Center (EPIC) monitors challenges to privacy, especially in the use of electronic databases and communications media, and publishes a yearly report on its activities, as well as other books and reports on the topic of privacy.

http://www.ftc.gov/bcp/edu/microsites/idtheft/index.html
The Federal Trade Commission's Identity Theft site is a one-stop resource for information about protecting yourself from identity theft and handling the problems that can occur if your identity is stolen. Features include an interactive game to test your online identity-protection skills.

http://www.heritage.org/research/homelanddefense/
The Heritage Foundation is a Washington, D.C., organization that issues reports on government and public policy issues. Its Homeland Security and Terrorism page contains links to the foundation's recommendations on antiterrorism policy, including statements on such topics as developing appropriate data-mining tools.

http://www.nyclu.org/stdt_main.html
The New York Civil Liberties Union maintains this page on students' rights, with information about court cases involving students' privacy and freedom of expression.

http://www.pbs.org/wgbh/pages/frontline/homefront/view/
Spying on the Home Front
This Web site is a companion to a 2007 PBS documentary about government espionage and surveillance of citizens in the age of terrorism.

http://www.privacyinternational.org/
Privacy International is an international human rights organization that focuses on government and corporate privacy intrusions around the world.

http://www.usdoj.gov/oip/04_7_1.html
This U.S. Department of Justice page is an overview of the Privacy Act of 1974.

http://www.whitehouse.gov/infocus/homeland/index.html
The Homeland Security page of the White House Web site contains presidential speeches and press releases related to antiterrorism efforts, defense, and immigration reform.

All Web sites were available and accurate when this book was sent to press.

Bibliography

Adams, Helen R. *Privacy in the 21st Century: Issues for Public, School, and Academic Libraries.* Westport, CT: Libraries Unlimited, 2005.

Barber, Benjamin R. *Fear's Empire: War, Terrorism, and Democracy.* New York: Norton, 2003.

Darmer, M. Katherine B., Robert M. Baird, and Stuart E. Rosenbaum, eds. *Civil Liberties vs. National Security in a Post-9/11 World.* Amherst, NY: Prometheus Books, 2004.

Dennis, Jill Callahan. *Privacy and Confidentiality of Health Information.* San Francisco, CA: Jossey-Bass and AHA Press, 2000.

Etzioni, Amitai. *How Patriotic Is the Patriot Act? Freedom Versus Security in an Age of Terrorism.* New York: Routledge, 2004.

———. *The Limits of Privacy.* New York: Basic Books, 1999.

Glenn, Richard A. *The Right to Privacy: Rights and Liberties Under the Law*. Santa Barbara, CA: ABC-CLIO, 2003.

Hentoff, Nat. *The War on the Bill of Rights and the Gathering Resistance*. New York: Seven Stories Press, 2003.

Holtzman, David H. *Privacy Lost: How Technology Is Endangering Your Privacy*. San Francisco, CA: Jossey-Bass, 2006.

Parenti, Christian. *The Soft Cage: Surveillance in America from Slavery to the War on Terror*. New York: Basic Books, 2003.

Rosen, Jeffrey. *The Naked Crowd: Reclaiming Security and Freedom in an Anxious Age*. New York: Random House, 2004.

Roth, Kenneth, and Minky Worden, eds. *Torture*. New York: New Press and Human Rights Watch, 2005.

Sykes, Charles J. *The End of Privacy*. New York: St. Martin's Press, 1999.

Index

Page numbers in **boldface** are illustrations, tables, and charts.

Afghanistan, 21
African Americans, 52–53
Agin, Patrick, 102–103
airport security
   baggage-screening, 79–80
   confiscated items, **11**
   racial profiling, 53–55
Al-Qaeda
   9/11 attacks, 13, 17
   camps in Afghanistan, 21
   and the Taliban, 21
   views by George W. Bush,
      14–16
America's Most Wanted, 70
Amnesty International, 61
*An Historical Review of
   the Constitution and
   Government of
   Pennsylvania*, 29

anthrax, 41–43
appropriation, 40
Arar, Maher, 67
Ashcroft, John, 18, 47
Attash, Waleed Mohammed
   bin, 64

Bethel School District v.
   Fraser, 101
Bill of Rights, 26–27, 31–21
bin Laden, Osama, 13, 21
biometric data, **45, 115,**
   118–119
bookstores, 50–51
border security, 20–21
Botsford, Clara, 37
Bowers v. *Hardwick*, 38
Brandeis, Louis, 32, **33,**
   34–35, 36–37

bullying, 111–112
Bush, George W., 81, 119
  speech on terrorism,
    14–16

Camp X-Ray, 60–62, **61**, 64
cell phones, 35
censorship, 101–103
Center for Democracy and
  Technology (CDT), 86
Central Intelligence Agency
  (CIA), 12, 45–46, 50,
    65–68
Chertoff, Michael, 43
City Journal, 20
civil liberties
  Bill of Rights, 25–32
  and the Patriot Act, 43–51
Civil War, 62–63
closed-circuit television
  (CCTV), 88–97, **89**
Combined DNA Index Sys
  tem (CODIS), 75
communication, 17, 46
Computer Assisted Passenger
  Prescreening System
  (CAPPS), 79–80
Coonerty, Neal, 50–51
cyberbullying, 111–112

Daschle, Tom, 41
data mining, 82–88
Department of Homeland
  Security (DHS), 17–20
Department of Motor
  Vehicles (DMV), 73
detention and detainees
  rights, 57–61, 64–68

Dinh, Viet, 43, 50
DNA information, 75–77
Douglas, William O., 38
Driver's Privacy Protection
  Act, 73
Drug Enforcement Agency
  (DEA), 84
drug testing, 105–109
"dumpster diving," 82
dystopia, 23

Eastman, George, 34
Electronic Privacy
  Information Center
  (EPIC), 76
enemy combatants, 59–61,
  64–68
Enlightenment, 25–26
Enquiry Concerning the
  Principles of Morals,
    29–30
ethnic profiling, 51–57

false light, 40
Federal Aviation
  Administration (FAA), 12
Federal Bureau of
  Investigations (FBI), 12,
  45–46, 50, 55-57, 71, 73
Federalists *vs.* Antifederalists,
  26–27
Federal Trade Commission
  (FTC), 120–121
Foreign Intelligence Surveil-
  lance Act (FISA), 44, 81
Franklin, Benjamin, 28–29
Freedom of Information Act
  (FOIA), 71–73, **72**

Gartenberg, Jim, 10
genetic information, 75–77
Genetic Information
    Nondiscrimination Act
    (GINA), 77
global positioning systems
    (GPS), 116, **117**
Gonzales, Alberto, 66
Great Britain, 89–91, 94–97
Griswold v. *Connecticut,*
    37–38
Guantánamo Bay, 57–61, 64

habeas corpus, 62–63
Hamdi, Yaser Esam, 64–65
Hamdi v. *Rumsfeld,* 64–65
Harvard Law Review, 32
Hazelwood School v.
    Kuhlmeier, 101–102
Health Insurance Portability
    and Accountability Act
    (HIPAA), 74–75
Holtzman, David H., 82
Hume, David, 29–30
Hussein, Saddam, 21

identity, mistaken, 67–68
identity theft, 119, 120–121,
    121
Immigration and
    Naturalization Service
    (INS), 20
immigration laws, 46
information providers,
    83–84
International Committee of
    the Red Cross, 61
International Emergency
    Economic Powers Act, 17

Internet communications,
    85–88, 109–112
intrusion, 40
Iraq, 21
Islamic extremists, 13, 17

Japanese Americans, 51–52
Juvenal, 82

Katz v. *United States,* 38–39
King, Martin Luther, Jr., 50
Korematsu v. *United States,*
    52
Kyllo v. *United States,* 77–78

Leahy, Patrick, 41
libraries, 50–51
Lincoln, Abraham, 62–63
Locke, John, 26

MacDonald, Heather, 20
marijuana, 77
marketers, 82–84
Mayfield, Brandon, 55–57,
    56
media and privacy, 34–35
medical information, 73–77
metal detectors, **104**
60 Minutes, 65–66
Mohammed, Khalid Sheikh,
    64
Morse v. *Frederick,* 102

nannycams, 92–93
National Security Agency
    (NSA), 81
Neier, Aryeh, 19–20
New Jersey v. *T.L.O.,*
    103–105

newspapers and privacy,
34–35
Nixon, Richard, 73

O'Connor, Sandra Day,
21–22
Office of National Drug
Control Policy (ONDCP),
107
Omar, Hady, 57–58
1984 (Orwell), 23, **24**
Orwell, George, 23

Padilla, José, 65
Padilla v. Rumsfeld, 65
Parenti, Christian, 70
Patriot Act
acronym, 22
amended, 68–69
introduction and uses of,
43–51
protestors, **19**
Sandra Day O'Connor's
observations after 9/11,
21–22
sunset provisions, 68
patriotism, 17
Pearl, Daniel, 64
photography, 34
Pledge of Allegiance, 99
police dog, **106**
postal workers, **42**
privacy
categories of privacy law,
39–40
and the law, 32, 36–40
laws and surveillance,
71–78
meaning of, 32

1984 (Orwell), 23
and security in the future,
113–123
and technology, 34–35
"The Right to Privacy,"
32–37
U.S. Constitution, 25
zones of, 38–39
Privacy Act, 73
*Privacy Lost: How
Technology Is
Endangering Your
Privacy*, 82
profiling, 51–57
protestors, **19**
publication of private facts,
40

racial profiling, 51–57
radio frequency
identification devices
(RFIDs), 116, 118
Real ID Act, 119, 122
Red Cross, 61
Roe v. Wade, 38
Rumsfeld, Donald, 64–65

Scalia, Antonin, 77–78
Schaefer, Rebecca, 73
Scheuer, Michael, 65–66
school safety and privacy
First Amendment rights,
99–103
Fourth Amendment rights,
103–109
Internet use, 109–112
searches and seizures,
103–109
Secure Flight, 80

Sensenbrenner, James, 44
September 11, 2001
    aftermath, 6
    Ground Zero, 11–12
    hijackers, 12–13
    impact on security v.
        privacy, 7–9
    Pentagon, 10
    United Flight 93, 10
    Washington, D.C., 10
    World Trade Center
        towers, 9–12
Sleigh, George, 9
Soft Cage, The, 70
spycams, 92–93
surveillance
    airport, 79–81
    data miners, 82–88
    domestic, 78–82
    privacy laws, 71–78
    video cameras, 88–97
    wiretapping, 81

Taliban, 21
technology
    and consumers, 82–84
    and foreigners, 45, 45
    and the future, 113–123
    and privacy, 34–35
terrorism
    Presidential speech on,
        14–16
    watch lists/no-fly lists,
        80–81
terrorist groups
    Al-Qaeda, 13, 17, 46
    freezing assets of, 17
    9/11 hijackers, 12–13

Terrorist Information and
    Prevention System (TIPS),
    78–79
Terrorist Information
    Awareness, 85
"The Right to Privacy,"
    32–37
Tinker, Mary Beth and John,
    100
Tinker v. Des Moines
    Independent School
    District, 99–101
torture, 59–61, 64–68
Total Information Awareness
    (TIA), 84
Transportation Safety
    Administration (TSA),
    53–54, 79–80
Two Treatises on
    Government, 26

Union Pacific Railway v.
    Botsford, 37
U.S. Constitution, 26–27,
    31–21, 62–63
U.S. Embassies, terrorist
    attacks on, 13
U.S. Treasury Department,
    45–46
U.S.S. Cole, 13, 64

Vernonia School District v.
    Acton, 107
video surveillance cameras,
    88–97
Vietnam War protest,
    99–101
visa violations, 57–59

Voice Over Internet Protocol
   (VOIP), 85

"War on Terror," 17, 78
Warren, Samuel, 32, 34–35,
   36–37
Watergate scandal, 73
Web sites, 132–133
*West Virginia State Board of
   Education v. Barnette*, 99
wiretapping, 81
writ of habeas corpus,
   62–63

About the Author

Rebecca Stefoff is the author of numerous nonfiction books for young adults. She has written about a variety of historical and scientific subjects as well as social and political issues. For the Supreme Court Milestones series, published by Benchmark Books, Stefoff has authored works on affirmative action and the death penalty. She also wrote *Marriage* for Benchmark's Open for Debate series. Stefoff lives in Portland, Oregon. Information about the author and her books for young adults is available at www.rebeccastefoff.com.